# Five Days Of Scenery

## Journey Across a Small Village

Mike Yanek

Author: Mike Yanek

Cover Design by: Anna Shledge

Copy-Edit by: Vicky Swann



ISBN – 978-1-9161925-0-8

Imprint: Independently published

Novel, historically inaccurate

www.mikeyanek.com

# Introduction

These are the personal writings of James Elmswood, an American journalist, who met and fell in love with the woman of his dreams, the beautiful Kalina, after she moved to the States to pursue her studies in higher education. Their romance blossomed, and after ten years of being together (five years married), it's time for the San Diego-based couple to visit Kalina's birthplace; a tiny village on the other side of the globe, located deep in the mountainous region of the Balkans (South-East Europe).

James' diary records all of his encounters over the five days he spent there in July of 1985.

# 07.22.1985 (Monday)

I heard a very loud, sharp noise, followed by my head slamming against the seat in front of me.

"Damn…What the hell?" I vocalized.

Looking around, I tried and gather my thoughts, and my brain whispered to me in a questioning yet hopeful manner, "Is this crazy bus ride finally over?"

I looked at my wife, who sat next to me, for more clues about what was happening. She looked happy and at peace… as usual, staring through the window. I didn't want to bother her, so I needed to find someone else to answer my questions.

As everyone around me was babbling in their own language, I knew where to look for guidance…the driver! That beacon of shining light. Oh, what a spectacle he was, immaculately covered in mesmerizing layers of the finest fabrics these lands could offer, tailored to perfection - a black track suit with white stripes. The top part was unzipped, and we were privileged to stand witnesses to this man's enormous belly and dense forest of black hair that saturated his vast chest. Keeping the jungle from spilling over was a thin white tank top, holding on for dear life, stretched to the maximum over the cannon ball that he was carrying under his chest. He had a round face, bushy eyebrows and a voice so deep, it sounded like it was coming from the center of the earth itself.

The driver was sitting sideways; this way, when the bus was not moving, he could face the passengers and join in on the communal experience, or just relax and take a break. His body was in an unusual pose. I wasn't sure if he had discovered, to quote my hippy cousin, "the enlightenment that is yoga," or whether he just wanted to do a lot of stuff at once and needed flexibility.

He had a dark beverage in a cup near him at all times. Judging by the way this man drove us, I was skeptical that this was simply some harmless apple juice, and decided it was more likely some sort of "courage enhancer." Even though I'm not a religious man at all, there were moments when I was secretly praying to the man upstairs.

"Oh God, I do hope this child of yours has only cold tea in that cup, not some sort of alcoholic concoction these people enjoy while driving."

I was saying those words silently whilst putting my hands together and looking up at the ceiling of the bus.

The driver had a magnificent meal spread out in front of him: the aforementioned plastic cup filled with the mysterious potion, accompanied by two big chunks of white cheese and a packet of really sketchy looking cigarettes. The three-star Michelin lunch was completed by a sandwich.

Even though I didn't have a front row seat to the breathtaking one-man show our multi-talented driver offered us, I still managed to visually dissect the masterful construction of his sandwich. I saw a complicated architectural and artistic endeavour. The man was the Michelangelo of his day – this was a multilayered combination of culinary ingredients, dancing, or may I even say flirting with each other, culminating in his greatest creation. Each layer was different from the other and yet weirdly fitting with each other; lettuce, huge pieces of tomatoes, a stack of an Italian-like salami, mini sausages, a few types of cheese and some red stuff that was definitely not ketchup.

"Oh no! Are you serious, my good man! Ray Croc, who we recently lost, will be spinning in his freshly dug grave!" my brain screamed in shock.

"Holding a sandwich with one hand!" I was shaken to my core. I was offended as an American; this was unacceptable! As I was nearly ready to say something out loud, my eyes quickly shifted upwards - just a few inches above this whole sandwich-eating fiasco. I looked away from the demolition of my culture that was unfolding right in front of my eyes, and noticed he was wearing one of those Irish *Donegal* caps.

"I haven't seen those caps around these parts. Maybe I am judging him too harshly. Maybe he is a bus driver who drives tourists across all of Europe. He probably bought that hat during one of those trips. Maybe he has seen lands I've never even heard of. What if he is a man full of sophistication; one who has tasted a multitude of cultures from the great buffet that our civilizations have to offer. A man that has enriched himself to a point that my own sometimes limited view of the world can't even comprehend."

As my beautiful thoughts were gently swirling through my mind and tempting me to believe them, a huge piece of tomato fell down from the colossal sandwich, right onto the driver's lap. Suddenly, he stopped his jabbering with the nearby passengers, and it took him a second to realize what had happened. He looked down, picked up the tomato, lifted it to eye level, inspected it for about two seconds, opened his big mouth and chucked it in with a vigorous and well-rehearsed move. A grin spread across his face, accompanied by loud chewing that resembled a woodchipper. He continued his conversation whilst devouring the remains of the sandwich with passion and ferociousness, at a progressively rapid pace.

My elaborate hypotheses and my beautiful imaginary account of his hat and the hidden culture this man possessed… yeah, that was all out the window now.

As I was sitting there trying to evaluate the driver's back story, analyzing and piecing his life together, I could not also address the symphonic background noise that had been traveling with us for the last four hours. I hadn't realized that such a small cassette player could introduce so much cacophony in my life. The composition, that is going to be the main soundtrack of my nightmares for weeks to come, is difficult to explain, for a few reasons. When it came to the lyrics, I had no idea what they were saying, unsure whether some of the artists were casting a medieval spell or serenading the girl next door. The instruments used in the track were not familiar to me; there were no overpowering violins, acoustic pianos or cello sounds.

"God, are those people banging sticks and rocks together?" a bigoted thought swiftly made its way to the top of my mind. I flicked it away and tried to be a bit more rational about it.

As I was trying to do that, it was hard not to be impressed by the volume of the performance that this little stereo was presenting us. The never-ending waves of foreign sounds blasting from that meager sound system didn't seem to bother the rest of the passengers. As I looked around, I confirmed my previous assumption that the bus was mostly full of gray old pensioners who were all very, very chatty. It reminded me of a retirement community down in Florida.

All of my internal monologues were interrupted by my wife's voice.

"Oh dear, we arrived!" she said with a huge smile on her face. "Are you ok?" she followed up. "You seem perplexed! Have you been having those over-analytical inner monologues again, dear?"

"Yeah," I replied. "Was I gone for too long?" I asked.

"Don't worry, it's all fine."

All of that gentle vocal poetry coming from my lovely wife was quickly interrupted by a loud command-like sentence in a language that I could not grasp for the life of me.

"BLADY-BLAA-BLA!" (this is how it sounded to me).

My wife instantly translated with an excited timbre to her voice: "We can leave the bus now," she explained as a huge smile spread across her face. "I think we can take our luggage now, oh, I can't wait!"

The reason my wife was so tremendously thrilled was because this was the first time I was going to meet her parents and spend a few days in the village that she was born and raised in; a tiny community that was located in the south-east part of Europe, a heavily dense mountainous region of the continent, referred to as the Balkans.

"Come, honey, let's stand up so we can move along to the front and leave the bus," Kalina exclaimed.

As we stood up, all of a sudden everyone was standing up as well; we were all jam packed into the tiny aisle.

"Oh great, it feels like a night club right now!" my mind signaled to me. It was hot, with too many people, loud music that I couldn't understand the lyrics of, and I didn't want to be here. Instead of being hemmed in by good-looking women in provocative clothes, I was surrounded by grandmothers carrying sausages, loaves of bread, big cubes of cheese and big glass jars of pickled vegetables in huge bags that had been strategically placed in the upper carry-on baggage space.

Moving forward with all these people around me was a slow and tedious process. As the driver was standing outside, right next to the door, and waiting for everyone to get out, he was waving his hand and talking to the passengers. I emerged out of the bus, carefully taking the two steps down. As my feet landed on the ground, the driver saw me, gave me a firm handshake and pulled me closer to him. He had a huge grin on his face and a sparkle in his eyes, and he confidently said something in his language. I imagine it was something like "See you soon." And as he opened his mouth to say that, an ungodly smell of the culinary architectural masterpiece that was the sandwich he had just finished eating not so long ago was emitted from his mouth. As he spoke his words of wisdom to me, his breath hit me like a frying pan in the face.

"Oh, c'mon! Really, use a mint for God's sake!" my internal thoughts immediately screamed.

I quickly let go of his hand and moved to the side. As I was waiting for my wife, who was just a few people behind me, I suddenly realized that this was the first time in the last four hours that I was standing up and moving outside of that bus. My body quickly felt that - I was sore, and I mean really sore! It felt like a group of nine-year old's had been hitting me with bamboo sticks for the last four hours. No fatal damage was done, but I felt like a considerable amount of pressure had been applied to my physique and I felt quite irritated.

The trip had been a hellish combination of lefts, rights and constant maneuvering. It had felt like trying to escape a maze with a reckless maniac as a driver. The road was primitive and damaged from years of neglect and heavy usage. However, I had to admit that, for a significant part of the journey, that was hard to notice, as the beautiful and scary scenery unfolded with every mile traveled. It had left me speechless a few times. On one side of the road, there was the mountain; on the other side, there was the "Grand Canyon's mini cousin", the "minor Canyon" - a scary and seemingly bottomless pit, created by the rivers and the movement of the rocks... or something like that. I knew I should have paid more attention in my geography classes back in high school. The only thing separating the right side of the road and the beginning of the pit was a little metal barrier, barely three feet tall and spanning as far as the eye could see.

This region of the world is very unfamiliar to me. I don't really know much about it. I know about my wife's city, where she spent her final years in high school and went to college, but that was located further north. The places here were different. This part was deep in the south; a tough chocolate-colored mountain region with only one main road leading to all the villages and medium-sized living communities that had the audacity to classify themselves as towns.

As my internal lecture was coming to an end, my wife came off the bus. She looked at me and said, "Did you enjoy the trip, my dear?"

I raised my eyebrows in a condescending manner and said, "What do you think?"

"Don't worry, you will enjoy your stay here, and you will absolutely love my parents, they are great!" she said with optimism in her voice. "Our luggage is ready. Let's wait in line here, and they will call our name."

As she was saying those words, I saw the driver opening up a secret-like compartment under the bus. He was calling out a name, followed by what I could only guess was a really funny joke, because everyone was laughing. He located the baggage and, for some reason, threw it to the side, instructing the passenger to collect his stuff. A weird ritual, I guess. We were all standing in a line that was moving very slowly. It felt like I was in line at the DMV or Post Office back home, minus the charming service, jokes and object tossing; well maybe the last one is not true.

We eventually managed to collect our belongings, and as we were sorting out our stuff, I lifted my eyes from the ground and… I saw it!

A big green sign with white letters…that I couldn't understand, because they all looked like someone got drunk and tried to re-write the English alphabet.

"Uh…my love," I said. "Can you tell me what does it say here? I have no idea what's happening. Is that a welcome sign, or some grandma's award-winning stew recipe?"

She giggled. "No, it's the official welcoming sign of the village," she continued. "Welcome to *Smilkja*, we hope you enjoy your stay."

"Hmm…interesting name…*Smilkja*," I said, as I was butchering the pronunciation of the village.

"No, honey," she corrected me, "the J is silent; it's pronounced *S-M-I-L-K-A*."

"Oh ok…I feel like I've become more cultured already."

As I was trying to be clever and a bit funny, the soft voice of Kalina was dancing around my ears as she said,

"Oh…look at the time" whilst looking at her watch. "I don't want us to be late. It's almost 4 o'clock! My parents are waiting for us, let's go."

As we headed towards her family house, I had a quick chance to visually scout the area. The village felt welcoming and cozy, snug in a way, like a bird's nest made of beautiful mountains, painted in the colors of peanuts and walnuts, with lush olive and sage colored forests, kissed by the sun, which was giving them a beautiful golden shade. A cold, dark blue river ran across the landscape, and fertile green fields were scattered around the area. A truly breathtaking scenery, the nature was definitely compensating for the fact that the village was not well engineered, with its slightly damaged roads, old houses here and there, and outdated facilities. It all had some charm to it, I must confess, but I could never see myself living here.

As I was drifting off into my mind once more, my wife spoke again.

"We are almost here. I can see the house."

When we got to the end of the road, I could see my wife's family home; the place where she grew up. It looked beautiful! Two stories, with two little terraces on the side, and two big terraces on the front; one on each floor. The windows were clear as day and framed by a smooth milk-white coating of paint. And there was the most colorful garden I had seen in a while, with a tidy thin fence protecting it from the local kids, who coincidentally might kick a soccer ball into the garden.

As we came closer to the house, I said to my wife, "Hold on dear…this garden is mesmerizing! Give me a minute."

"Ok, honey, have a look around…I will go to the house and call my parents. We will be in front of the main door downstairs," she said and gave me a quick kiss on the cheek, then swiftly made her way to the house.

While I was standing near the fence, I had a full look at this gardening masterpiece. It looked like an artist had been using the soil as his blank canvas to paint a picture, and he had completed his work in such a beautiful and aesthetically pleasing way. It was a tsunami of colors, like a Mardi Gras parade, only without the whorish women and the filth. A vivid yet orderly orchestra of all sorts of hues, flowers and arrangements. A wonder of the village world.

On one side were all the flowers, lined up in military fashion, saluting the sun with layers of saturated colors: lemon yellow, indigo blue, tiger orange, egg-shell white, wine purple, crocodile green and mahogany red all wrestling with each other over who wants to be the most visible and most revered in this garden. A battle of a lifetime!

Separating them was a little concrete pathway. On the other side, there were rows, radiant in red pastel shades, of strawberries and raspberries. The light breeze that had accompanied me and my wife so far, was gently moving the heavy strawberries in a synchronized motion - a picture to behold. It looked like they were flirtatiously waving at the raspberries, who were located, as if playing hard to get, right across from them.

This scene culminated with a stoic apple tree, confidently sitting at the end of the garden. Its location was fit for the king of the area, as it truly was, overlooking its loyal servants and protecting its kingdom.

An old righteous tree with perfectly shaped apples that possessed an irresistible glow. Fruit so…

"James!" My inner thoughts were interrupted. "Come, dear, my parents are waiting for you."

I saw my wife had opened the main gate and was shouting from forty yards away.

"Ok, James, it's time to meet your wife's parents!" I was self-coaching in a reassuring voice. "It's now or never. Just relax, and it will be fine."

As I was walking the short distance, my heart started to beat faster, my palms became moist and my anxieties started to kick in. Since I didn't have time to reflect inside my head on what was happening, before I knew it, I was in front of the gate. My wife opened the door and greeted me, giving me a hug.

"James, meet my parents!"

So, there we were, me and him - Kalina's father - looking at each other. He was at the end of the short path that lead to the house, no more than fifteen yards away from where I was standing. It felt like we were recreating a Clint Eastwood movie scene - two cowboys standing alone in the middle of a dirt road in a tiny godforsaken town in the Wild West. The music becomes intense, all the shop keepers close their windows and the kids and women hide and watch from a safe distance as they anticipate a duel to the death. There is a close-up shot of the eyes, then the camera switches to the other cowboy, who is smoking a cigar, trying to predict his opponent's next move. Yes, that was the exact feeling I had; that moment was capsuled in my mind.

Her dad was a man in his late 60s. He was of average height, perhaps 5'9", had a snow-white hair with a big bushy salt-and-pepper beard. He was in his white tank-top, work shorts and boots, he was a man that looked masculine, tough and agile, despite his age.

We started to walk towards each other, as if to say, "The first cycle of mutual judgement is complete, let's move to phase two." We were a handshake away from each other, so I extended my hand and, with a trembling voice, said, "James! Nice to meet you."
He grabbed my palm and applied pressure; it felt like a vice was crushing it, a hand that was used mostly for writing and drawing. His mouth opened, he collided his eyebrows into a frown and said, "Marko," followed by a few mumbling sounds that I didn't understand.

My wife interrupted and jumped in to draw us apart, like a boxing referee who tries to break up two fighters that are clinching too much.

"James, honey…my father says his name is Marko, and he is very happy to meet you and welcomes you to his house," she explained.

As I was reading his body language; his posture, facial expressions and the fact that he had tried to turn my hand into dust; I was not really sure if the translation that my lovely wife had provided was absolutely accurate. But I just rolled with it.

"Oh, thank you…please translate that my name is James Elmswood, and I'm very happy to be here and I'm looking forward to spending the next few days in their village and home." I looked at my wife.

As she was interpreting to her father, I was respectfully standing there, not knowing where to put my hands or what to do. The old man was listening to the gentle words of Kalina and looking at me, staring me down like a hawk. After she finished translating, he just nodded in a way that spoke to me, "I agree with those words, but I still don't like you."

Kalina then said, "Oh James, here comes my mom!"

And there she was, the mother of my wife. A woman in her mid…

"Aargh!" The noise I made as the air suddenly left my lungs. My inner dialog was cut short by a huge strong hug from Kalina's mother; an embrace even my own parents haven't offered me for the 42 years I've been on this planet.

"My name is James, nice to meet you." I said while being smooshed by this overly affectionate woman.

She started shouting in her language while rocking me from left to right. She seemed so overly excited, bursting with energy and ecstatic to meet me.

"She said her name is Ginka, and she is so happy to finally meet you," my wife translated while laughing. "She has heard so much about you."

After a few minutes or so, the unofficial greeting ceremony was coming to a close, as Kalina's mother hadn't taken a single breath while bombarding me with foreign speech, in a very positive tone, I might add. I started to feel a bit awkward; a recurring theme of this trip so far.

I must acknowledge that the house had an interesting entrance; a little gate followed by a few yards of concrete pathway, and on the right side a massive staircase made out of solid granite. You needed to climb the stairs so you could earn your reward and enter this beautiful residence.

A few moments later, we sorted out the bags and walked up the stairs. All standing in front of a beautiful wooden engraved door, my wife announced, "Welcome to my childhood home, dear!"

As we walked in, a sense of coziness, comfort and love wrapped around me instantly!

"Please take your shoes off," my spouse translated.

"Excuse me, what? Take my shoes off?!" I said with a surprised ring to my voice.

"Yes, it's tradition," Kalina said.

As I was taking my shoes off, my wife's mother opened a little door, strategically located right next to the stairway that led to the first floor. She pulled out some sort of homemade footwear, made out of thin wool, in a form that resembled *panini* bread, but in a bunch of colors that didn't go with one another. Orange, baby blue, dark green and black, and lots of it.

"Here you go, put them on. I want to see how you look," my wife said as she extended her hands, holding this masterpiece of color coordination.

I put them on…instantly my wife's mother clapped her hands and said something in an optimistic and upbeat voice.

"Perfect!" Kalina translated.

"Do you feel like you're walking on sunshine right now?" my wife asked me.

"I think I do," I replied as we all started to laugh. I was a spectacle at that moment.

So, there I was, feeling so cozy and comfortable in my brand new…

"Ugh, dear…what's the name of those things?" I asked, pointing down to my feet.

"*Terlucjki*," she said with fluent pronunciation.

"T-E-L-U-K-I" I said, hoping I got at least some part of the word correct.

"The correct pronunciation is T-E-R-L-U-C-K-I," she confirmed.

"I'm learning already, right?" I said, slightly lifting my eyebrows.

Her mother was nodding with a big smile.

"Where is your father?" I asked, as I felt too much approval and needed somebody to give me a grunt or a bad look.

"He's probably working in the garden outside," Kalina said. "My father will join us later. Let's relax and have some coffee now," she suggested and took us to one of the rooms that was at the end of the short corridor.

We walked into a small guest space. Even though the area was pocket sized, it had character. It felt like a bird's nest, surrounded by family pictures. It had a big window with thin sheer drapes, a modest terrace that overlooked the garden, a dining table big enough to fit four people, and a single bed shying away in the corner. As you walked in, there was a big wooden drawer on your right side with a radio on top of it, and a few steps further to your left was the hidden gem of this intimate environment, behind a thick brown curtain…a magnificent tiny kitchen.

The kitchen was equipped with a warm oven for baking cookies and pies, and right next to it, on the left side, a medium-sized sink to wash the fruit picked from the garden outside. Next to it was a small countertop, and at the other end, a white medium-sized fridge. To top it all off, there was a window no bigger than an A3 sheet of paper, right above the oven, giving you a direct view of the beautiful dance that the mountains and forests had been exhibiting for centuries. A front row seat to the beauty that nature provided those villagers on a daily basis.

"This is delightful," I said, as I couldn't stop looking around the room.

"You haven't seen anything yet, dear. This is the place where we have coffee and make food from time to time," my wife informed me with a smile on her face. "Wait until you see the rest of the house later on."

Kalina's mother prepared some tea and coffee for us in the kitchen, while me and my wife sat down.

"Oh, looks lovely…please sit down and join us, Mrs…ugh!" I looked to my wife and said, "Mrs. Ivan, right? Like your old surname?"

Kalina nodded in approval.

"Mrs. Ivan," I confidently finished off my sentence.

She raised her hand and stormed off to the big chest of drawers across from the table; a massive dark-brown, hand-made creation. Half of it looked like a set of sock drawers with four identically sized compartments, one above the other. On the other side of this wooden structure was a door with a gold-ish key in it.

"Oh wow, a golden key, and a door that needs to be locked?" I said with a high density of sarcasm in my voice. "What's so priceless behind that door? Gold bars…? Diamonds…? Secret chicken recipe…?"

"Even better!" Kalina replied.

"Click," the door of the cabinet started to open, and Ginka was about to review one of the most astonishing compartments I'd ever seen. Once the door was fully open, a gold-ish glow hit my face… I swear that I heard little angels singing gospel music.

"Oh, my God!" I said, with my mouth wide open. "Can I go and look up close, even maybe touch it?" I asked, while gawking at my wife.

"Of course you can! That's why it's there," my love said.

I moved closer to inspect the miracle that had unfolded before my eyes. I was in heaven…so much…candy and booze! A big compartment divided in to three levels and organized to perfection.

"I don't know what makes me happier right now," I said, while sitting near the cabinet and turning my head to Kalina. "How much candy and alcohol is in here, or how perfectly organized this cabinet is."

"Have fun, dear! That's why you're here," she said, while waving one hand and holding a cup of coffee in the other, and talking to her mother at the table.

I felt like a little boy in a candy store.

"Oh, they have a shelf for each category…no way!" I said to myself in a childish voice. "A shelf for salty snacks, a shelf for sweets and, most importantly, a shelf for…alcohol!"

There was an elaborate arrangement on each shelf, full of unfamiliar treats. Top level – oh, what a glorious display of salty goodness! In the background, cheerfully waving and greeting, were four bags of short yellow puffs of different flavors. Even though the writing on each packet was foreign, the mystery was quickly solved, as the pictures of a salt shaker, a stick of butter, herbs and a few slices of bacon told me exactly what seasoning those blond fellas were drowning in.

Right in front of them were a wide range of bags of all shapes and sizes; red packets with brown sticks covered in salt, green packs with medium-sized baked donut-shaped pieces of bread with a variety of seasoning, and yellow bags with a medley of small crackers of different shapes with a picture of cheese on the front.

This collection was accompanied by six medium-sized sachets; three on each side of the shelf, and each pouch was filled with nuts that were familiar to my native land. Two bags of each; peanuts, cashews and almonds.

The whole exhibition was completed by the center stage piece; a medium-sized box of home-made hard pastry in the shape of straight pretzels.

The visual tour continued as my eyes moved downwards, and it was time to dive into the center of this world of wonders and delight. The middle shelf was all about sugar. A mixture of boxes, mostly narrow and long, were located on both sides of the shelf space, with beautiful pictures sprawled all over them, telling the story of how these confectionery gifts came into existence.

Inside the cartons, the treats were covered mostly with chocolate. They came in all shapes and sizes: triangles, squares and circles with holes in the middle, resembling flat donuts, and a few more oddly-shaped sugar-covered surprises.

Ceremoniously sitting on top of all these were an army of individually wrapped wafers, covered with a thick layer of caramel or chocolate, with a heavy sprinkling of peanuts or hazelnuts.

The central space was permanently occupied by three elegant and beautiful flat boxes filled with the appropriate amount of chocolate pieces.

In the shadows of this overwhelming frontal display…a mixture of colorful candy was shying away from the spotlight, providing the worthiest background imaginable. Individually-wrapped strawberry and blueberry sweets, a vast amount of bubble gum packs and a few lollipops were doing their job correctly.

And now it was time to move to the main event of the day…the bottom shelf…the alcohol! I was anticipating a familiar sight, maybe some French champagne or some nice Italian wine, but unfortunately, I was struck by the unfamiliarity I experienced. There were three tall bottles, full of golden liquid of a slightly dusky shade, dark green water imprisoned in two stagnant and obese bottles, followed by a squad of miniature flasks, constructed out of glass with an orange cap, no labels and a transparent drink trapped inside. The center of this shelf was dominated by a massive thick jug, filled to the brim with a flowing substance the color of dark mahogany wood, that I was praying was wine, but I was not sure.

As I was looking around, confused and dazed, a familiar friend was being timorous way in the back. A face that I recognized made itself known…an average-sized bottle of gin! The bottle label had writing and all sorts of verification's on it… all in English! Finally, something that I was actually not afraid to take a sip out of!

"This looks amazing!" I exclaimed to the hostess.

She went to the kitchen and got a few small plates and bowls.

I went back to the table and had a few sips of delicious home-made peppermint tea, calming my excitement.

In no time, the table was filled with a seemingly endless variety of traditional snacks that I had familiarized myself with just a few minutes earlier.

I turned to my wife and said, "I want to talk to your mother. I want to get to know about her life and this village. Will you do all the translation back and forth, dear?"

"Of course I will," Kalina said with a smile.

Even though me and my wife have been married for five years, I only know a bit about her parents and the village, but I could never remember the names of the locations, the details and the years correctly, so I decided to get the information straight from the source.

"So, Mrs. Ivan, how did you meet your husband, Marko?" I started off the conversation.

"They met in her hometown; a small mining community located roughly 13 kilometers east of *Smilkja*. The name of the town is *Rodadjem*," my wife was retelling her answers and translating. She continued, "He used to work as a miner there for more than, twenty years and she was working as a dispatcher near the mines, so this is how they met."

"Sounds interesting!" I exclaimed. "A woman working near the mines; that's something you don't see very often."

"Oh yes, she is one tough cookie," Kalina said while looking at her mother and giving her a big smile.

"How long have you lived in this village then?" I continued my investigation.

"She and my father moved here when they both retired from the mines, thirteen years ago."

All the time I was looking at this old lady and thinking, "This woman was working for such a long time in the most intimidating environment ever...a mining community, surrounded by brute and tough men…giving them orders, telling them where to go to search for precious metals, bossing them around, not taking crap from anyone. And yet she is so gentle, kind and sweet to everyone, treating all like family…now, that is a strong woman right there! And now I know where Kalina gets her fearlessness and kindness from…"

"You have a lovely home," I slightly changed the subject and threw in a compliment.

"Oh, c'mon dear, house tour! House tour!" my love exclaimed, jumping up.

Before I knew it, me and my wife were standing up and heading out of the room. Her mother started putting the uneaten snacks in containers and cleaning up the dishes.

As we were in the small corridor in front of the room, I felt like I was in a museum, and my wife was the tour guide.

"The house was built in 1970," my spouse informed me. "Built by Marko and his two best friends from his mining days."

"What?! Three people built this house, all by themselves?!" I enquired with a great disbelief in my voice.  .

"Please don't interrupt the narration of this guided tour, thank you!" Kalina said with a sneaky smile, and gave me a wink. "The house has two main floors and a huge basement. Today, we will look at the floor we are currently occupying and the floor above it," she continued in her broadcasting voice. "To your right, we have a staircase."

I raised my hand

"Yes sir," she said while pointing at me.

"Stairway to heaven?" I asked, trying to be clever.

"Very inappropriate, sir," she replied while trying to stay in character.

"Let's go to the left now."

We headed in that direction. We were in a small corridor again with three doors; front, left and right.

"To the right, we have a bathroom," she pointed, while we headed straight on.

We opened the door and entered a new area. "As you can see here, we have a big study room," she gestured, waving her hand around to describe the size and importance of this space.

And what a space that was! When you walked in, on your left side, there was a snow-white wall engraved with fine details from top to bottom. Back home, we have wallpapers covering our walls, but this was different; a beautiful series of shapes, patterns and designs chasing each other around the open field that was this wall.

To the right of the entrance door, there was an old light-brown handcrafted cabinet, full of dusty vintage books; a homemade library in a sense.

I quickly stepped from the guided tour of the house museum. I raised my finger and said, "Just give me a minute, please," as I bent over slightly, trying to scan the literature for some familiar authors.

All the hardbacks were in their own language, so I didn't understand any of the titles. The books were clearly old and many in quantity.

Right in front of the wooden structure, there was a big couch, covered in thin plastic to keep it clean and fresh. At the end, there was a smaller armchair in the same design, again with a slender cover. To top it all off, there was a small table in front of the two pieces of furniture, covered with a substantial white cloth and with a beautiful plant standing on top of it.

On the other side of the room, there was another timber cabinet with some books, notepads, souvenirs, family pictures and documents.

All around the area there were plants and flowers in pots. The finishing touch was a big terrace located opposite the entrance door.

I took a mental picture of this ensemble, as this reminded me of my shrinks office.

"Sorry for going off the guided tour," I apologized to my chaperon, as she was still in character. "I guess this room is all finished," I stated as I did a semi-spin to see if I could manage to visually scan everything. "Shall we move to the next place?" I suggested.

"There is one more part of this room," Kalina said as she approached a secret door that was located at the end of the vast white wall. "The bedroom!" she exclaimed and opened the door, inviting me to take a peek into a medium-sized area with a girthy bed and one modest wardrobe in the corner.

"Oh wow, looks great!" I said with a smile on my face. "So, this is where me and my lovely wife will sleep?"

"Oh no, honey," Kalina broke character for a bit and continued, "my parents are very traditional, and we will have to sleep in separate rooms."

"Hold on… what?!" I said with disbelief in my voice. "Oh c'mon, are you serious?!"

"Sorry, those are the house rules," she said and quickly jumped back into character. "And now… for the floor upstairs!" she cheerfully shrieked, while holding my hand and dragging me out of the room.

As she was overflowing with positive energy as usual, I was moaning and complaining…as always. We passed the door that was opposite the bathroom, and I said, "Hey, how about this room? Why are we skipping this one?"

"This is for last; this is the dessert!" she said.

We ended up on the first floor, where there were two corridors; one to the left, and one in front of us.

"And now, ladies and gentlemen, please follow me, as we are going straight to the storage room," my wife announced, pretending to maintain order and signal to a large group of old imaginary tourists.

I raised my hand.

"Yes, you sir," Kalina said while pointing at me.

"Can we take pictures of that room?" I asked.

"No, you can't!" she surprised me with her answer and continued, "But no worries, we have laminated posters down at the gift shop."

I started laughing at her being creative and silly again, then went for a spontaneous kiss, as I couldn't help myself.

"Please sir! I barely know you!" she declared, tilting her head to avoid my kiss, still portraying the character that she had come up with twenty minutes ago. "I'm not that type of tour guide you know…Now, if you look to your right, you will see…," she continued like nothing had happened.

Those little quirks in her personality are the reason I'm crazy about this woman. She is definitely the opposite of me. Where she finds the energy to be so positive, care-free and always up to something fun, I do not know. Unlike me… just leave me alone with some good gin and tonic, some quiet Dean Martin whispering his greatest hits in the background, and let me write and draw all day… that's heaven for me.

As I started to realize that I'd zoned out again, I quickly snapped out of it and paid attention to what my tour guide was saying.

"To the right, we have a little kitchen, equipped with an oven, fridge, sink and a cabinet," Kalina said. "We continue our tour by entering the preparations room, which is straight ahead," she finished off her sentence.

As the door opened, I saw a medium-sized space that looked more like a section of a downtown grocery store back in San Diego than a place where people can live or even stay for more than twenty minutes. The room was filled with big bags of green, yellow and red apples. There were all types of herbs and teas on top of old newspapers, left to dry on the floor, as well as big sacks of chestnuts and walnuts, and a whole cabinet and shelves filled out with big and bright yellow quince fruit.

This little improvised grocery store was supplemented by a large terrace, decorated with a few plants and flowers in pots, and there was a tiny white plastic table with two emerald-green camping chairs.

Just as I thought that the tour of this room was finished, my lovely tour guide opened yet another secret door. I took a quick peek at this small space, and it was filled with boxes, personal belongings, some old family pictures, documents, memorabilia and some books. I don't know why, but this room felt way too private and personal; it didn't seem appropriate to snoop around, so I closed the door after about thirty seconds of looking inside.

"Let's make our way to the rest of the floor, ladies and gents," Kalina, who was fully committing to her comedy character, said.

As we got out of the storage area and passed the little improvised kitchen, we turned right and headed to the room that was at the end of a long corridor.

We entered a decent sized space, resembling an average living room…a sofa, armchair, solid table, a cabinet with a radio on top and a small fire stove in the corner were the main participants in this assembly. The area was complete with a small kitchen to one side and a tiny terrace overlooking the charming garden to the other.

A small curtain casually blended the living area with a small bedroom.

My visual senses were not stimulated, as the rooms looked dull and ordinary… but I remained polite and said "Oh, looks lovely!"

"That almost concludes our house tour!" she said. "And since you've been such a great audience, it's time to go and see the last room, located downstairs!" my wife pronounced, springing into action, and saying, "Follow me!"

We made our way downstairs… Standing in front of the mystery space, I was feeling excited, due to the fact that our lovely tour guide had been building up an air of suspense and mystery regarding this place for the last thirty minutes.

Kalina opened the door and said "Ta-dah!"

"Oh my God!" I exclaimed with my eyebrows raised and my pupils widening. "This is absolutely beautiful… I'm speechless!"

It was a substantial room with so much detail, impressive craftsmanship, and adorned with ornaments that I couldn't comprehend it all at once. The creativity and skill that had been poured into this area was beyond anything I'd seen so far.

All the walls were covered with thin wooden boards that had been carved and polished to perfection…with some sort of mosaic constructed out of colorful pebbles at the very bottom.

Covering the ligneous surface were a few small and medium-sized handmade cloths, saturated in all colors imaginable, and for some strange reason, the material was attached to the walls. The symmetry of the shapes and the color combination made the odd decoration truly stand out.

A thin yet sturdy wooden shelf was running across the top part of the walls, with many bite-sized ornaments, souvenirs, hand-made gifts and a few family pictures proudly standing on top of it.

On the left side of the room was a small cinnamon-brown table with a delightful handcrafted yellow fabric casually relaxing on top, a few beautiful red roses in a transparent blue-tinted vase, accompanied by some family pictures and souvenirs.

Towering in the background was a cabinet; a colossal wooden construction with many different parts, that was covering the entire wall. There were a few little windows on some of the compartments, and inside you could see the graceful presence of crystal glasses, shiny silverware and blue and white porcelain plates…used only when special guests were around or just for display; who knows.

On the lower half of the cabinet, there was a huge black and white TV, smack bang in the middle.

"This construction looks amazing! Reminds me of something you would find in a trendy vintage store in the West Coast," I said while my mouth was half open in awe.

"Please direct your attention to the very top," said my tour guide.

There was a medium-sized stuffed eagle on a tree branch with his wings open and his beak ready to attack.

"Oh my God!" I uttered as I put my hand to my mouth. "I didn't expect that," I said in a state of shock and confusion. "You're not supposed to have a stuffed animal in your room, let alone an eagle."

"Sir," my wife, who was giving an Oscar-worthy performance so far, said. "This type of room is called *bitova*, and it's traditional around these parts of the mountain region. All the decoration, style, and even a stuffed animal is very authentic and normal for this kind of space, I assure you," she explained, reading from her imaginary clipboard that she was pretending to hold in front of her.

I continued my visual tour across the room. The wall that was directly opposite the entrance was almost entirely occupied by a huge window with long and thin drapes, which were strewn with never-ending flower designs and shapes. The room was engaged in a vicious stare-down with the surrounding mountains and forests, and you had the privilege of a front row seat every time you stepped inside and guided your attention to that massive window… the scenery outside was breathtaking.

Most of the area was occupied by two long and narrow tables that were connected to one another. All around them were benches covered in hand-made traditional cushions and sitting pads. These tables looked sturdy and ready to handle many celebratory occasions.

In the right corner of the room, there was a small fireplace, covered with a beautiful design of marble and pebble pieces on both sides, and with a white chimney.

"A fireplace?" I asked my tour guide in surprise.

"Oh, yes sir, even though it's warm and very enjoyable during the day, especially in summer, like it is now, the evenings can get chilly around these parts."

I nodded in agreement.

"And that, ladies and gentlemen, concludes our guided tour of the house, thank you," she announced while she took a small bow.

"That was great, well done!" I said, clapping and cheering.

I heard Kalina's mother calling her from the other room.

"Oh dear, what time it is?" she said, and took a look at her wristwatch. "It's almost 7 o'clock. It's time for dinner!"

I was quickly instructed to just relax and watch TV.

"Dinner will be served in about twenty minutes, dear," my wife said and gave me a kiss on the cheek, then hurried off to the next room to help her mother with the food.

"Do you want me to help you with something?" I asked Kalina as she was leaving.

"Don't worry, take it easy, you're our guest," she said as her voice and body were moving away.

I headed straight to the TV; a big intimidating piece of machinery. It was a dark-brown box with a big screen, with seven small red-ish buttons located on the right corner and a very big bright-red switch next to them.

I started the TV, white noise first came on the screen, followed by a sound that reminded me of a laser being shot in a sci-fi movie. Then the entertainment came on... some sort of weird talk-show with a host in a cheap suit, sitting across from another man in a cheap suit. They were babbling about God knows what; politics, foreign affairs, breast sizes and the male obsession with them, I don't know, I'm just guessing.

Right at that moment, the door that was almost closed started to open.

"Honey, can you translate what these people are talking about?" I asked, while slowly turning my head, as I was expecting Kalina to enter in a few seconds.

I heard a grunt.

"Sorry, can you repeat, dear," I asked, as my peripheral vision was not clear. I needed to completely turn around. "Oh, sorry Mr. Ivan," I said with a slightly embarrassed look on my face. "I thought it was Kalina," I finished.

Her father was finally back in the house. He was carrying several small logs of wood for the fireplace. He started to quickly arrange the firewood, eventually setting them on fire… controlling the flame with just a few moves and some sheets of old newspaper thrown in for good measure; a process that this man could do in his sleep from the skill and routine that he had developed from doing this thousands of times.

As he was preparing the fire, Kalina and Ginka walked in with the first batch of culinary goodness, and as the distance between the two rooms was very short, the food kept coming in at a very fast pace.

About fifteen minutes later, we were all sitting at the table. As usual, my eyes were dancing across the gastronomic display; the sheer amount of deliciousness that was presented to me made me feel like a judge at a culinary competition. Food so unique and unfamiliar to me, that it was impossible to try to figure it out or describe it. Also, I was definitely not in the mood to analyze it, since my stomach was hauling from starvation.

It was time to dig into this mountain of traditional dishes. Before we started, we needed to partake in the international tradition… we each took a hold of our beautifully engraved crystal glasses, raised them up, looked at each other and said in a synchronized voice, "Salute!" Our glasses collided and made a loud clinking sound.

The food was abundant, the wine sweet and tasty, and the atmosphere was cozy. Me and Kalina were talking and laughing, and she was translating as I was trying to talk to her mother as much as I could.

Her father was not receptive to my attempts to try and have a conversation with him, as he was stuck in his ways, I guess.

After about two hours of pleasantries in a snug family atmosphere that I was very happily surprised that I had enjoyed so much, the dinner was over.

My wife and her mother started to remove the plates, put the food away and clean the tables. As she was pacing back and forth with dishes and food in her hands, Kalina said, "Your room will be ready in about twenty minutes, dear." She added, "And I know you are a night owl, but you'd better get some sleep; people wake up pretty early around these parts."

I was feeling tired from that crazy bus ride, so I agreed, "Yes, I will get ready and hit the sack in a bit, thanks dear."

In the bathroom, located across from the *bitova* room where we had been having the feast of a lifetime, I brushed my teeth and washed my face. I heard the smooth voice of my wife, signaling that my room was ready and that everyone was about to go to bed soon.

I was going to be staying in the small guest room; the same space where we'd had tea and coffee earlier that day Kalina was going to sleep in the big bedroom next to the reading space on the same floor, while her parents would be snoozing upstairs.

As I headed to my accommodation, I bumped into Kalina in the small corridor right in front of my room. I wrapped my arms around her waist and held her close, leaning in for a big kiss. As I came closer, she pulled away and cleared her throat while lifting both her eyebrows and pointing her petite nose just behind my right shoulder.

I turned my head around and saw both of her parents standing right at the end of the corridor. I quickly remembered that Kalina's mother and father came from a more traditional culture, and I thought that it would be inappropriate if her parents were to see me kissing her... Marko staring at me didn't help either... I suddenly panicked, swiftly pulled away, then raised my hand and gave her a handshake!

As I was moving her hand up and down, I stumbled over my speech and said, "Well... Mrs. Elmswood, that was a great meal! And you are a worthy travel companion...yes you are?!" My brain was going into autopilot, and I was saying the first words that came to my mind.

Kalina started giggling quietly, lifting both her eyebrows again, and slightly shaking her head from left to right, she whispered, "You're such a silly idiot sometimes...I love you."

She let go of my hand and went to her parents, gave them both a goodnight kiss, and before she went to her room, she turned around and said to me, "And you... Mr.

Elmswood, I think it's time for you to go to bed now…goodnight!"

Her parents waved at me goodnight; well, only her mother did; her father just raised his right eyebrow and gave me a dirty look. They both went upstairs, and Kalina headed to her bedroom.

I went to my room and changed into my pyjamas. A thought was bouncing off the walls of my brain: "I will rest for thirty minutes, wait until her parents are asleep, then sneak into the bedroom and see her!"

I laid on the single bed… that mattress felt like somebody had carved off a piece of heaven and glued it to the most comfortable and fluffy cloud that you could find around these parts. I fell deeply asleep in about ten minutes…so much for sneaking out to my wife's room…

# 07.23.1985 (Tuesday)

"COCK-A-DOODLE-DOO!!!"
"COCK-A-DOODLE-DOO!!!"
"COCK-A-DOODLE-DOO!!!"
My heavy eyelids slowly raised and eventually opened as an unbelievably loud sound pierced my eardrums.

"What the hell is going on? What's that racket?" I muttered under my nose.

As I looked beside the bed, there was a small battery-powered alarm clock.

"Oh c'mon…it's seven in the morning…for God's sake!" I said grudgingly.

The intense noise continued, but I managed to locate the source; I went to the little kitchen that was across from the bed, and I took a peek out of the small window above the oven. There it was…the perpetrator of all this rumpus…a chicken coop on one side of the vegetable field, which was property of the house. And at the front of the henhouse, a proud and arrogant rooster was singing his heart out.

I opened the window and yelled, "Hey you! Shut up! Can't you see what time it is? See how early it is!" I went off on a rant while clenching my fist and shaking it in the air. "Some people are trying to sleep over here, God damn it!" I shouted.

The rooster stopped his serenade of the village, turned his head around, lowered his forehead, gave me a disapproving look, then quickly turned his head back to its original stance… and crowed even louder!

I closed the window, as I realized that I wouldn't be able to negotiate a few more hours of peaceful sleep with this crazy bird. I poured myself a cup of fresh cold water from the tap at the sink and leaned against the wall. As I was refreshing myself and trying to wake up, I heard a bunch of loud noises coming from the room next door.

"Ah, now what?!" I grunted.

Placing the glass on the kitchen counter, I headed out of the room to investigate what was happening. A few steps later, I was standing in front of the main guest room. I opened the door and saw my wife and her parents sitting and having breakfast.

"Morning, sleepy head!" my wife hollered above the volume of the TV, which was turned to its maximum capabilities.

This was not a big surprise for me, since Kalina's parents were up there in age, and their hearing was getting worse I suppose.

"Err…morning!" I shouted, while holding my hands over my ears to signal that the TV was too loud. "Can we turn down the volume?!" I screamed at my wife.

"What? Turn up the volume?" she yelled back. "I think it's loud enough, dear!"

At this point, I started to mimic what I was trying to convey. It looked like I was playing charades at 7:15 in the morning, half asleep, with messy hair, and in my pajamas, jumping and pointing to the TV like a maniac, to the accompaniment of a morning talk-show in a foreign language.

"Ah, turn down the volume!" my wife said, finally solving the visual puzzle I was presenting.

Kalina quickly made her way to the TV, and a few moments later, the talk-show was at a reasonable volume.

I placed both my hands on my waist, and with a shortness in my breath, I said, "Good morning everybody!” I did a little beauty pageant wave with my left hand and gave them a fake smile.

As I sat down, I was greeted by everyone. Well, mostly by my wife and her mother; the old man ignored me a bit. Shortly, an empty plate was presented to me.

“This is how it works here, dear,” my spouse instructed me. “It’s a bit of a buffet; you pick and choose whatever you want from these big plates of food. Do you want me to sort out your dish and make you a traditional breakfast?” she asked while lifting my empty plate and casually hovering it in the direction of the four big ones.

“Sounds like fun, yes please!” I said eagerly.

A few moments later my plate was covered with authentic, or so I was told, breakfast. Kalina placed my dish in front of me, and I looked at it very analytically.

“Ugh, honey…you sure this is the type of stuff people eat around these parts? It doesn't really make sense, to be honest,” I said, while giving her a puzzled look. “Who eats olives and pickles for breakfast?” I asked, while giggling slightly and trying to hide my amusement at the same time. “Oh no…why is there salami on my plate? And wait, what is this big white soft cube over here?” I enquired, while pointing to one side of my plate.

“Goat cheese,” said Kalina.

“Goat cheese?!” I was shocked. “Pickles, salami, olives and goat cheese!” I will just have some tea or coffee and toast, I’m fine really.

“Ok, Mr. Big City Man!” my wife exclaimed in a playful tone. “You see that jar over there?” she said, while pointing to the end of the table. “That is called *Lutenkja*, but I call it “heaven in a jar.” I will make you some, and you tell me if you want to continue having breakfast with us, or have your precious tea…deal?" she offered, while extending her right hand.

"Deal!" I said, while shaking it.

"Watch and learn, Mr. Hollywood!" she exclaimed.

"Oh c'mon, Kalina…you know I don't come from Los Angeles. I'm from San Diego, born and bred, and very proud of that fact!" I said, lecturing her in a playful voice.

"Yeah, yeah, yeah… open this jar, because it's sealed," she said, while laughing and handing it over.

After a few attempts and a few chuckles from my wife and her mother, which didn't do wonders for my ego, I managed to open it.

"Watch and learn, big boy!" she said, grabbing a slice of white fluffy bread and winking at me.

Kalina grabbed a butter knife and took a big scoop of the red paste from inside the thick container, then a fairly even coat of the secret ingredients, which had pesto-like consistency, was spread all over the toast. She took a pinch of spices from a tiny bowl located nearby, sprinkled them with such precision, then reached for the big white cube.

"Hold on!" I said. "Is that the goat cheese?" I asked, while squinting my eyes in disapproval.

"I will use cheese made out of cow milk, ok?" she asked me. "You will like it, I promise."

She took a few small pieces and placed them on the bread.

"My masterpiece is complete!" she said, while putting the creation on my plate. "Try it out," she offered, while pouring some hot peppermint tea in the cup nearby.

I picked up the toast and took a bite. An explosion of flavors rushed vigorously into my mouth. No more than ten seconds in… and my taste palate quickly started to recognize most of the ingredients. The grilled red peppers were the leading actors in this play, brilliantly supported by the understudies... the tomatoes and chili peppers. The spices were creating an intense tornado... exuding a delightful aroma; parsley, basil, thyme, black pepper... all accompanied by garlic. And on top of all that, the white cheese, with its smooth, strong and slightly bitter flavor, was completing an exceptional experience in my mouth.

"Wow...this is amazing!" I said to Kalina with my cheeks full, while I was chewing; I looked like a hamster!

"I know, right?" she said with raised eyebrows.

She prepared a few more slices for me and her parents. I washed the toast down with some tea and water.

The time was sprinting, and before I knew it, breakfast was over. It was around 10am according to my wristwatch.

As Kalina and her mother started to clear the table, I leaned back and relaxed on the padded bench area that surrounded the table. While my wife was running up and down with dishes and food in her hands, I looked at her and said, "Oh, let me help you with that!"

"You relax for now," she replied. "Me and my mom will need to start cooking in a bit."

"What, more cooking?" I asked.

"Yes dear, there is a huge festival in a few days, and everyone will be there. A lot of people from the neighboring towns and villages come as well, and we need to be prepared," Kalina explained while pacing around.

"Oh, really? What type of food do you need to cook?" I asked.

"Mostly cakes, cookies and jams," she said. "Relax for a bit, because I think we are short on a few ingredients, and we may need your help. I will check and will be back in a bit."

"Ok, take your time. I will be in here."

Kalina left the room and went to talk with her mother, while I was once again drawn to the simple beauty of this tiny living community. I went to the massive window that occupied a substantial part of a wall, looking outside and admiring the colorfully dense forests that were covering the stoic dark mountains. Scenery like that had a positive effect on me; I needed more nature in my life, as being stuck in a cubical inside of a gloomy gray, concrete building back home is not something that works great on a person's creativity and mental state.

"James!" I turned around and saw my wife had reappeared. "Ok dear," she said, "we lack a few ingredients, so we will need your help."

"No problem! I will go to the shop," I said with confidence in my voice. "I would love to see how people partake in commerce and discover how retail operates around these parts."

"What shop?!" Kalina started chuckling. "There are no shops in this village!"

"What? No shops?! How do these people survive?" I asked.

"Everyone produces something to consume. If you don't produce, someone else in the village most likely will," she informed me while gesturing and explaining. "If no one is making it, you go without."

"Without?! What?!" I was stunned. "So, no Count Chocula corn flakes?"

"No," said Kalina while shaking her head.

"So, no deliciously orange, crunchy Cheetos?" I asked, suspiciously squinting my eyes.

"No," my wife answered with the same expression.

"Ok, hold on!" I said, putting both my hands up in the air. "Please tell me that you at least have gummy bears in this village?"

"Oh, yes, of course we do!" said Kalina with a dubious amount of irony, that was positively snowballing, in her voice. "Our oldest resident in the village is Grandma Magda. She is 94 years old, and when she is not feeding the animals, working on the farm, or relaxing in front of the TV, watching her favorite soap opera, whilst knitting *terlucjki* for her grandchildren, she has created a mini production line in her basement, so she can make gummy bears!" The level of sarcasm in my wife's voice was reaching the size of a huge wave.

"Does she really have a gummy bear factory in her basement?" I asked, raising my eyebrows, whilst smooshing my lips and tilting my head slightly to the left.

"Of course not!" said Kalina as her tsunami of sarcasm flooded the whole room.

"Well…she should!" I said, while slightly nodding my head and squinting my eyes. "It sounds like a solid business plan, you know! I think a lot of people would enjoy the health benefits of gummy bears… Also, if she is the only manufacturer, that means no competition…boom, profits! This is how it works, you know!" I believed every word that came out of my mouth.

"You are too much sometimes!" my love said, laughing. "There are plenty of shops in the towns and cities up north. Once a week people go there with their trucks and buy essentials that nobody can produce, or that they can't find locally," she explained and quickly continued. "Ok, listen here, big city man, we need you to do a job, see!" Kalina said, squinting her left eye, creating a finger gun, pointing it at me and dressing up her voice in an accent that resembled a Chicago gangster from the 1920's.

"Who do you want me to mug, boss?" I asked, while trying to play along, but my accent was not even close to being as good as hers. I definitely lacked the improvisational skills and the comedy timing that she was gifted with.

"No Mugsy!" she stayed in character and was now pretending to smoke a cigar. "We have an even bigger job for you. See the neighbor's house right opposite the garden over there?" She pointed her imaginary cigar to a little bricked den that was just a few yards away.

"I see, boss! What do you want me to do to this kid?" I asked with my budget version of a mafia accent.

"You go to his place. Knock on the door," she instructed.

"And then…I whack him, right?" I exclaimed.

"No Mugsy, you ask him for two cups of sugar, one cup of vegetable oil and some butter!" she said, while adjusting her imaginary fedora, which she had just added to her fictional outfit.

"Oh, but does this person speak any English?" I asked, completely breaking character.

"Yes, he does. He's a young guy who speaks very good English, don't worry," my spouse said, snapping back from her time-traveling Mafioso guise. "Please go and help us out today, as we are really busy."

"Oh, I see how busy you are, Mrs. Capone; running an organized crime syndicate and making jam and cookies on the side is not easy!" I said, while chuckling a bit.

Kalina laughed, gave me a hug and a kiss, then left the room to go and help her mother with the baking and preparations for the event that was just a few days away.

I quickly changed from my pajamas into some home-wear. I put my sports shoes on and headed out.

A minute or so later, I was in front of this mystery person's place. From the outside, his living accommodation seemed very strange, as his house didn't look properly finished. The brickwork skeleton was visible, as there was no paint job; just orange and red cinder blocks, connected with fine layers of concrete. It looked ugly and weird.

I knocked on the solid red, wooden door that was in front of me, took a few steps back, and a moment or so later, the door slowly opened, making a loud irritating sound.

"Namaste!" said a peculiar looking man, who put his hands together, raised them to chest level and took a little bow.

"Ugh…Hi there?!" I said, feeling immensely confused and surprised.

"Oh, an English-speaking soul," he said in a suiting tone.

"Soul? Err…no, my name is James." I gave him a suspicious look, followed by my extended hand.

"I don't believe in handshakes, brother," he said.

"Hugs is the only currency I deal in."

Before I knew it, he had sprung forward like a wild cheetah attacking his pray, and he gave me a big hug. Rocking me from left to right, he started whispering in my ear, "Let the free flow of energy transmit between us, my kin."

"Ugh…what…no?!" I quickly managed to escape his embrace. "I don't know what is happening here, and this whole brother, kin, energy nonsense is freaking me out!" I raised my voice. "I'm just here to pick up some sugar, butter and oil. Can I please have some, so I can be on my way!"

"Come in!" he said with a big smile on his face.

"Oh God, do I have to?" I exhaled, while hoping that this was all just a practical joke, and that he would break from this character that he was playing ever so well.

"My brother…you are not on the path of enlightenment yet…but that is ok, as we all need time to grow. We are like little plants in the garden of life and…"

"Ok, ok, I'm coming, I'm coming!" I quickly interrupted him, as I couldn't bear to hear where all this absurdity was headed.

As I took a couple of steps in, a thick fog of unusual smells wafted around my face, like a cheap scarf on a windy day; a mixture of scented candles, aromatized bamboo sticks and salami… all smothered in a heavy blanket of ganja fumes.

I was moving very slowly and cautiously inside a place that was hard to explain. My mind couldn't grasp the interior design that this man had constructed or hired someone to complete, but hadn't finished. There was a big, almost empty space, which was the living room, I supposed. It was covered with thick wool rugs and lots of scatter cushions all over the place, a hefty amount of scented bougies, dirty dishes piled up in one corner, a small radio cassette player, lots of pictures of him and his family, I presumed, traveling around the world, and posters of some sort of psychedelic visual sensations that would get you high just by looking at them.

On the left side, there was a small kitchen with only a sink, tiny fridge and a cooking stove, and a mountain of unclean plates, cutlery and cups all over the place.

Next to the kitchen was a door that was half open. It looked like this was the bathroom, with an old bathtub and a few buckets full of water, together with washing detergent and a few pairs of socks and underwear hanging nearby.

"Oh God, this man doesn't even have a washing machine," I hastily spoke to myself as I was looking around to confirm my observation. A few moments later, I realized I was correct! This man lived a life of complete savagery. I couldn't comprehend such a lifestyle. I couldn't live this way!

"Make yourself feel at home," the host said as he waved his hand in a very welcoming manner.

"Oh, thank you for the hospitality, but can I just have the ingredients and go?" My voice was trembling.

"Yeah, sure. But come in…you know," he said with a big grin on his face.

I was hesitant to move any further into this parallel universe…I was not sure what I was about to get myself into. I had no idea what was wrong with this man; his looks, his speech and the living space that he was occupying were absolutely alien to me; a behavior and lifestyle I couldn't partake in, even in my wildest nightmares.

"Ok, I'll stay, but just for five minutes, and then I really need to go, ok?" I said, as I felt that he was onto me, and I didn't want to seem rude or insulting.

"Cool!" he said, giggling. "Oh man, take your shoes off, yeah?"

"Oh, ugh, can I keep them on? I'm stepping on concrete here," I said, as his house didn't have any type of wooden flooring or any sort of protection. There were only a few small rugs scattered all around the place.

"This is a shoe-free zone, brother…use my flip-flops," he offered, pointing to the dirtiest hippie sandals I'd ever seen.

"Yeah…I think I'll pass, I'm ok," I said, taking my shoes off and stepping on the cold concrete in my white socks.

He was sitting in a yoga position at the end of the room on a big shag, surrounded by little pillows, smiling and waiting for me to join him.

"Come, have a seat," he said in a tranquil voice.

"Yeah, sure," I said as I came closer to the little cushion haven that he had created for himself. "Do you have a chair?" I asked.

"Chair? Why do you need a chair when Mother Earth is your chair?" he said as he pointed to the ground near him.

My eye roll was so loud, I think I woke up the cattle at the end of the village. "Who says things like that? God, this guy is pretentious!" my mind was screaming.

After a quick struggle to reposition my body into a pose that is apparently known in the hippie community as "the lotus," I managed to successfully mimic the sitting posture that this eccentric person had adopted in front of me.

As I was sitting opposite him, there was a heavy shroud of silence all around us. I couldn't help but visually scan this man's unusual physical appearance; a skinny guy with a truly bizarre haircut. He was bald on the top and at the front, with a bit of hair to the sides and loads at the back, pulled into a ponytail, then tied in a knot; a hairstyle I'd never seen in my life, at least not in person. His head was big, like a watermelon, with small eyes, a large nose and thin lips, and he had two piercings on each ear. His complexion was pale as the goat cheese I almost had for breakfast.

"Can I have my ingredients now?" I asked out of the blue, as the pause was becoming excruciatingly long and painful.

"Yeah, of course," he said, while staring at me and not moving a muscle.

We just sat there. He didn't stand up or anything, so I just decided to try and have some sort of a conversation with this human mystery.

"So…your English is really good," I said in a very optimistic voice, trying desperately to start an exchange of some sort.

"Oh yeah, because, you know…I've traveled and I studied back in the day…I come from the capital, *Serdikja*, way up north. It's different there." He started talking, even though there were many gaps and odd pauses in his delivery. He was giggling in a bizarre way. It was a bit complicated to follow his pattern of verbal expression.

"Oh, so you're not from the village?" I asked in a surprised tone. "How long have you been here?"

"Hmm…my body…about five years…my soul, a bit longer."

I didn't even attempt to ask and get an explanation regarding that "soul" comment, I just plowed ahead like things were going normally.

"Oh, very nice, what made you move here, from the big city to such a tiny place?"

"You know what…" he took a deep breath, "soil is more important than concrete," he said as he was exhaling, and then continued. "In soil, my brother, everything grows; dreams, hopes, love, passion, purity and, most importantly, life…while on concrete, only greed, hate, desperation and pollution thrives."

I completely lost his train of thought. At that point, I was just waiting for him to finish speaking so I could ask him another question.

"Oh yes, yes…very interesting. I completely agree with what you said." I was nodding with a blank look on my face.

"So, what do you do for a living? How do you get by in here?" I asked him.

"I do odd jobs here and there…painting somebody's house, a bit of blacksmith or locksmith work, driving a tractor…"

"Oh, interesting, do you get many job offers and projects?" I asked him curiously.

"Zero so far," he replied with the same half lost-in-the-clouds, half serious look that he'd been offering me so far.

Looking at his living conditions, it kinda made sense that nobody wanted to hire him. I started to wonder how this man survived if he had no job. I couldn't help myself and asked, "So…how do you get by? If you don't have a job?"

"Oh, hmm…" he slowly mumbled as he was looking up at the ceiling, visually searching for something up there. "I grow vegetables…fruit. I trade supplies with the locals, and my parents are filthy rich," he finished, giggling.

"Your parents are rich?" I repeated with a look of
shock on my face.

"Yes…my parents are brainwashed and are caught up
in the corporate system, you know…poor people! My
father is a lawyer, and my mother is a physician….Ha!
What a waste of time!" he concluded with a loud burst of
laughter.

I was truly surprised. The more I got to know this
man's backstory, the weirder this whole experience was
becoming.

"Oh…that's fascinating!" I said, leaning in ever so
slightly. My body was subconsciously revealing a higher
level of interest; much more than I'd expected.

"So, what do you think about…"

"JAMES!!" I heard my name being screamed
repeatedly.

"Excuse me for just a moment," I said to the odd guy.

I found the nearest window, opened it and poked my
head out of it. Kalina was standing on the first-floor
terrace of her house.

"James, are you coming? Did you get the ingredients?
We need them now!" Kalina was shouting.

I looked at my watch. "I've been here for two hours!"
my voice soared in shock. "How is this possible? I
thought that I'd only spent ten minutes in here!" I
exclaimed, while gesturing to the sitting man. "This place
is like a parallel universe…makes you lose track of time,"
I said in a joking voice.

"This is the parallel universe…my brother," he said
with a suiting timbre.

"Ok…and it got weird again," I said, putting both my
hands on my hips. "Ok…buddy, I really need those

ingredients now, because the women are cooking, and they need my help," I said.

"Well…my brother…the univ…"

"I don't have time for this!" I said out loud.

I picked this small man up and took him to the kitchen, which was a few feet away. While in the air, with his legs still wrapped around one another, he was surprisingly calm, and still talking in that weird manner. I put him on the kitchen counter, still in the lotus position. He was muttering some spiritual bullshit, so I interrupted him with an increasing urgency in my voice.

"Can I have the ingredients now, please?!" I asked, lifting both my eyebrows and looking at him.

His face was just blank, and his lips were mumbling some odd phrases. This man had reached his nirvana, I guessed.

"Ok…just point to where you keep them," I said, as I was losing my patience.

While still rambling and completely lost in his thoughts, the odd dude pointed to the top shelf of a small cupboard and then a small fridge. I quickly collected what I needed, then found a white grocery bag that was casually laying on the floor, so I put everything inside.

"Ok…buddy, it was nice meeting you…now I have to go!" I said, while looking at him still sitting on the kitchen counter.

But before I left, my curiosity got the better of me, and I blurted out a question.

"What's your name, by the way?"

"Drozdan…" He snapped out of his trance and replied with a smile on his face.

I extended my hand to shake his, as is the custom when you learn someone's name…but he quickly made me withdraw that extended palm… wanting a hug, with his arms wide open, while still remaining in that yoga position on top of the counter, surrounded by an army of dirty dishes… That was not my idea of an introduction.

"Err…nice to meet you, take care!" I said, while slowly moving away and heading towards the front door.

As I was walking, I caught a blur in my peripheral vision on the left side. I needed to go, but my curiosity couldn't let me leave without finding out what that muddy spot was.

I turned my head, and at the top of the staircase that led to a small bedroom, I saw… proudly standing there… covered in all shades of blue with big splashes of orange and red… a medium-sized rooster.

"Why is he in your house? He needs to be outside in the coop with all the other chickens," I stated, while pointing at the little fella.

"That's my pet rooster," Drozdan said, while lovingly looking at his companion.

"Ugh…of course it is," I exhaled, performing an eye roll. "Ok," I said in a defeated tone, "tell me…what's his name?"

"Gagarin!" he said.

"Gagarin?" I fired back with surprise.

"Yes…like, you know…the first man in space," he concluded.

"Oh…God!" I burst out laughing.

I wasn't sure what did it for me; whether it was the thick ganja fumes, the psychedelic posters or the heavy cascade of bullshit in the form of theories about the universe that this man had showered me with in the last two hours… I couldn't hold my laughter any longer. It was spilling all over the room at this point.

"That's enough for today, Drozdan…I need to go now…Nice to meet you, and have a great day!" I said, while walking away and shaking my head slightly, then looking up.

I put my shoes back on, as my feet were freezing from the cold concrete floor, and my white socks had turned gray from all the dirt. I opened the front door, and the fresh breeze caressed my face while the sunshine gently waved at me.

"I completed my quest!" I announced to myself happily as I was finally headed back to Kalina, so I could proudly display my gatherings.

While I was walking, my mind was vibrating from the experience that had just occurred. People like that don't usually cross my path in life. I couldn't stop thinking about all the things this man had said. Had I just gone through a life-changing experience? Or had I just lost two hours of my life listening to a crazy person? I was perplexed… Was there more to life than just chasing a career? Or was this man just bitter that his parents were so successful, and he probably couldn't cut it in the ruthless world of high-level professionals. Could you really live with almost nothing, producing your own food, in an unfinished house, barely enjoying any modern-day luxuries, and still be really happy? Or was this man just so self-medicated that he didn't know what was happening around him?

My mind was now working at full speed, trying to analyze this man. I couldn't stop thinking about his lifestyle and where his happiness came from?

Was this man disingenuous? Did he pretend to be happy and calm, or was he really that way? Or maybe he was like all of us… broken, alone and unhappy with a few brief moments of joy…

Before I knew it, I was knocking on the front door of my wife's house.

A few moments later, I was greeted by the love of my life… her beautiful smile followed by her soft voice saying, "Hey…look who's back…with everything we need!"

I completely snapped out of my inner dialog, analyzing the meaning of life. I extended my arms with the white grocery bag in my hands and quickly responded, "Well…that was a trip of a lifetime!"

"He's a really sweet boy, that Drozdan, right?" My wife said, this time offering zero sarcasm or comic relief in her voice. "You know, when we correspond with my mother, she always says good things about that man. I've never met him, as he is relatively new to the village, but he sounds like so much fun…right?" she said.

"Well…ugh…I don't know where to start with that guy…," I said, shaking my head.

"Oh…I think somebody made a new friend today…," Kalina teased, while laughing and poking me in the stomach with her left index finger, for some reason.

"Oh…can I just hide somewhere and relax for a bit…I'm tired already," I said, giving my wife the cutest look I could muster.

"Of course…we are in the kitchen upstairs, cooking. Find a quiet place and relax. I'm sure there is no work for now that we need your help with," she said, waving goodbye and heading upstairs.

I went to the little guest room, where I had been sleeping previously.

"It's time for James to get a drink…too much craziness today," I said to myself, while opening the three levels of heaven contained in the left side of that wooden cabinet.

"Gin…where are you? Let's see…" I hovered my finger over the bottom shelf where all the booze was group-hugging. "Here we go…that looks like it!" I said as I picked out a bottle that strongly resembled my favorite alcoholic drink. "Tonic…show yourself…rise before me…my dear!" I said out loud as I raised my left hand slowly and spoke with a deep made-up voice. "I think I found the tonic!" I yelled with a smile on my face.

I gathered the main ingredients that I had found so far and headed to the tiny kitchen nearby. I picked out a tall crystal-clear glass, put it on the counter to the left of the sink, looked around, and yes… a fridge…right opposite that cute mini oven.

A swift movement on my part, and the fridge door was open. The yellow-ish light from the bulb inside gently hugged my tired face. All the compartments in the fridge were jam packed with food, and right at the top, there was a freezer box. A few seconds later, the small white door was wide open, and my eyes were scanning everything inside. Yes… in the corner were two ice cube trays.

I pulled out one of the trays, placed it next to the glass and the two bottles of magic liquid. My journey inside the fridge then continued. I was looking at the two cream-colored food boxes at the bottom that needed to be pulled out so that the contents could be reviewed. Compartment on the left… pull… full of veggies! No good! Compartment on the right… pull… fruit! Apples, grapes, bananas and peaches were all wrestling with one another, and in the corner, shying away from all of this madness… a lime and lemon… jackpot!

Rescuing them from all the havoc that they had probably witnessed for a few days, I gave them a thorough five-star wash.

Seconds later, a chopping board was on the counter, and a samurai-sharp knife was in my left hand. With a few swift moves, the single small lime and half a lemon were cut into precise pieces. The rest of the lemon was put away in the fridge, and the knife and chopping board ware quickly showered and stored away.

The green and yellow pieces of fruit were dropped into the bottom of the long glass, followed by the crackling of five small ice cubes, mercilessly hunted down by a horde of gin and tonic… My beautiful creation was complete!

I expeditiously made my way out onto the small terrace, which was attached to the outside of the room. "Hmm…this is too small; I can barely fit a chair here…hmm." As I was thinking out loud, my attention was snatched by that crazy guy who I'd spent two hours talking to earlier that day. He was outside his front door, sitting in the lotus position, meditating.

"Nope…I'm not looking at him while I'm trying to relax! Not a chance!"
I said and promptly moved off the terrace. "I think there was a balcony on the other side of the house on this floor?"

A moment or so later, I was in front of the big terrace that was attached to the study room.

"Ah, this will do!" I said with a smile on my face, as the area was spacious enough, and even had a dark-green fisherman's chair. "Ah…finally!" I exhaled loudly, throwing my tired body onto the seat.

In front of me, there was a farm and a house, which were not that interesting, but behind them and to the left were the mountains and forests; a running theme of my stay in the village so far.

As I was slowly lifting my slim glass of heavenly juice to my mouth, whilst enjoying the dazzling landscape, the sparkling tonic was shooting tiny cannon balls of bubbles at my lips, and the gentle crackle of the ice cubes caressed my ears. When the brim of the glass was only an inch or two away from my mouth, my brain was anticipating the path my body was about to go down for the thousandth time…

"James!!" A loud scream brutally slashed the flavor ceremony that was about to unfold.

"James, where are you?" my wife was yelling.

"Oh, God…what now?" I was forced to put down my drink and slowly stand from my chair.

"Oh, here you are!" Kalina said with a surprised look on her face. "We need you! My father is digging out potatoes in the vegetable field outside, and he needs some help," she finished, while grabbing my hand. "Oh, you made gin and tonic! Can I have it?" she asked, scooping my drink from the floor.

"Well…I made it for me, but you know…" I mumbled.

"Thanks honey!" she exclaimed, while taking a sip.

Moments later, we ended up in front of the potato field, which was attached to the beautiful fruit garden. I was given working boots and gloves, and after quickly changing, I got a pat on the back from my wife as she said, "Have fun dear!"

She went upstairs while finishing off my drink, which I never even got the chance to taste.

What followed was me pretty much holding various potato sacks for a grumpy old guy, who was muttering in a foreign language whilst digging out root vegetables and casually throwing them near me. I was convinced that he was aiming for my head, but I didn't have enough evidence to prove it. Fun times!

After an hour of the unpaid manual labor that was requested of me, we finally finished, just at the right point, I might add, as it was time for lunch.

We headed upstairs to find Kalina and her mother already sitting in the small guest room, where I had been sleeping. They were eating some sort of stew, bursting with all types of meats and vegetables, accompanied with a salad and a few other small traditional dishes, with delicious white and puffy slices of bread.

An hour or so later, I was full and happy. Lunch was over, and I couldn't wait to finally hide away somewhere for a quick nap or just to relax with a cold drink in my hand. As I remembered that there was a big couch next to the window in the study room, I promptly excused myself from the table and made my way there.

"Ah…look at that!" I uttered at the sight of the sun softly patting the burgundy leather surface of the couch next to the big window overlooking the mountains and forest. "Oh…would you look at that! A blanket as well!" I said out loud, while picking up a piece of light cloth located on one side of the couch.

Just a few precise moves later, and I was laying on the firm surface of the warm couch, covering myself with a thin layer of soft fabric that resembled a cloud plucked from heaven.

My eyelids felt heavy, and it only took a few moments for me to doze off. Before I knew it, I was asleep.

"James…James, honey!" I opened my eyes very slowly and saw the blurred image of my wife's face just a foot away from mine. "Wake up honey, we need your help!" she called.

Usually I was quite pleased when the first thing I saw was Kalina's face when I opened my eyes. But not this time. I just wanted a few minutes of peace and quiet for myself.

"Hey…is everything ok?" I slowly managed to get the words out of my mouth.

"My father needs your help. I'll be in the main guest room waiting for you," she finished, then left the room.

"Oh, God damn it! Now what!" I said while trying to wriggle my way off that comfortable couch.

After a minute or so, I was up and ready to go. I quickly folded the blanket, fixed my hair and washed my face in the bathroom nearby.

"Ok, I'm here now. Is everything ok?" I asked when I entered the main guest room.

"Ok dear… my father is outside the house all ready to go," Kalina said.

"Ready to go where?" I asked.

"To the woods," she replied.

"Why does he need to go to the woods?" I queried suspiciously.

"To pick berries… we are making jam. We are starting this evening, and we will finish off tomorrow," she explained while lifting a cup of coffee from the table. "You see, we've done most of the cooking, so we are on a break now…but we need some freshly picked wild berries from the woods for a few more cakes and mainly for the jam that we need to prepare for the big festival that is coming up," she smiled and concluded.

"Hold on…the woods?!" my voice wavered. "You want me to go with your father to the woods?" I was in shock.

"Don't worry, it will be fine," Kalina tried to calm me down.

"But you grow berries in the garden," I tried to defend my case, pointing out the window straight to the section where they had all the red and burgundy fruit.

"I know, but that is not enough…please, be a dear and help him out," she pleaded, while giving me a charming smile that I couldn't resist.

"Oh…ok, what's the worst that could happen, right?" I said, chuckling and lifting my shoulders.

The old man was waiting in front of the gate when I went to join him a few moments later. We started walking towards the woods. I knew this was going to be an awkward experience for both of us, since there was no way to communicate. I had the feeling that this man still didn't like me. Was it because I'm married to his daughter, because I'm foreign or maybe because I don't really participate in physical labor back home? I'm not sure. I think he sees me as a gentle and soft person, coming from a generation or part of the world that indulges in fast food, booze and selfishness. I think he sees me as a man with no values, no core, no strength, or maybe he's intimidated by my appearance, intelligence and my mind…

"Why are we stopping here?" I hastily interrupted my inner thoughts with a layer of surprise.

"Drozdan!" the old man yelled in a very commanding tone.

A big bald head popped out the window.

"I'm so happy to see you, James!" said the bizarre person, who I'd met only that morning, while quickly opening the window near to his door.

His attitude resembled that of a Tibetan Buddhist, so "the happy monk" was a nickname that popped into my head… it would suit him well!

After a little while, he was standing in front of us, dressed in work boots, a sweatshirt and overalls. He jumped and gave me one of those big welcoming hugs that he loves dishing out, like candy on Halloween.

"I will be joining you…for this trip of a lifetime…my brother!" He said out loud, while hugging me tightly.

"Ok…ok…can you please let me go now, Drozdan!" I said, trying to escape his clutch.

After a few moments of struggling, I managed to free myself from the grip of this crazy man. Marko was standing to one side, slowly shaking his head from left to right and scratching his intimidating, thick beard.

"Why are you coming with us?" I asked the happy monk… I couldn't help myself.

"Because, you know…you need a spiritual guide…and your in-laws asked me to come, so I could keep you company and translate for you as well…" he smiled.

"Oh, that is very sweet of you, minus the spiritual guide thing; that's just weird," I thanked him.

"And to fight off the bears," he said, displaying a serious look.

"The bears?!!!" I jumped. "You have bears in these woods?!" I couldn't believe it.

"Who said anything about bears, my brother?" Drozdan was surprised.

"You did!" I screamed, while pointing at him.

"I don't know anything about the bears!" He lifted his shoulders and started walking with the old man towards a narrow pathway.

"Aren't you going to close your window and lock your front door, Drozdan?" I asked while following them a few steps behind.

"Nobody will steal anything, no problem," he said while moving forwards.

"Yeah, with all that crap you have inside, who would bother wasting their time robbing you?!" I mumbled very quietly under my breath.

"What?" the happy monk asked.

"Nothing, nothing," I replied, while pacing behind both of them.

After a few minutes of walking, we found ourselves at the side of the river that was not far from the house; a picturesque, stoic and experienced, medium-sized creek, seemingly shallow at first glance, but I had a suspicion that this creation of mother nature should not be underestimated in any way. The middle of the creek looked dark and unwelcoming, while the banks looked bright and friendly, smiling and waving us in, to come and enjoy a relaxing dip.

Nearby was a skinny bridge that looked primitive and untrustworthy. Its wooden boards, splashed in mocha brown, were resting next to each other, bonded together with a very thick rope that seemed strong enough, but I couldn't afford to invest my full trust in it.

"Err...is there another way to cross the river?" I asked, while pointing at the crude bridge.

"It will be fine, my brother. The universe has a plan for us, you know…we will go into mother nature and pick her fruit…" the happy monk spoke softly as he was making his way towards the bridge.

"Oh, universe… if you really have a plan for me…can you strike me with lightning or something…but please do it soon…I would not be able to survive a few hours with this lunatic in the woods…picking berries and listening to his views on you, the universe!" I muttered to myself while shaking my head in disbelief.

Marko and Drozdan marched with giant confident strides over the frail construction. I finally gathered the courage to follow them. As I took the first few steps, I thought to myself, "Oh, this is not that bad." I didn't even have the chance to finish my sentence, when I felt the wooden boards start to vibrate and shake beneath my feet…the whole structure started to swing from left to right.

"What is happening?!!!" I yelled in a panic.

I looked up and saw Drozdan at the other end of the bridge, with a huge grin on his face from ear to ear, holding the two ropes that were supposed to provide some sort of a safety railing, and swinging and shaking the construction.

"What are you doing?!!!" My body filled with horror. I yelled at him, "I'm going to fall and die…!" I was terrified.

"The universe is protecting you…my brother…you will never fall…" Drozdan was howling with laughter.

"What if the universe is in a bad mood today…and her superpowers can't defend me?!" I yelled back at him, while holding on for dear life with both hands on the ropes.

"Well…what day is it today?!" he was screaming like a maniac; something that was unusual for him. He was standing at the end of the bridge, while I was stuck in the middle, right over the deepest part of the river, having a full-blown panic attack.

"Today is Tuesday!" I screamed back.

"Oh…the universe has a day off today, I think!" he said with zero irony.

"Please, stop shaking the ropes and rocking the bridge! I will fall into the water!" I yelled.

"Don't worry, the fish in the river are very friendly!" he replied.

"How the hell do you know that?!" I fired back.

"I talk to them…from time to time," he replied loudly yet calmly.

At this point, Marko had enough; he was not very fond of pranks, shenanigans and people just playing around. He went over to the guy who was causing all the havoc and started talking to him in a commanding voice, then only a few moments later, the bridge was calm again. They both started walking towards the tiny grassy hill up ahead.

I was forced to rapidly compose myself and to chase them down; I was so bad at orientation that I would probably have ended up lost within a few seconds if I was by myself. I quickly forgot about the terror that the happy monk had just caused me, as there were too many other distractions and so much overwhelming nature all around.

When we had descended the jade-colored elevation, a dense green region of trees was visible on the horizon, signaling the beginning of the woods. A minuscule pathway, which had been carved out by humans, allowed for an expedient entrance into the forest. My attention was immediately seized by the sight of a wooden cabin to the left, right in front of the trees.

Unfortunately, I didn't have the chance to visually analyze this structure or even ask about the backstory of this visibly occupied living space,
because the old man and the bizarre guy were fiercely moving towards the berries that were in the woods, supposedly.

As we passed deeper and deeper into the forest, Kalina's father was pointing to the different trees and explaining something very specific about the classification and type of leaves of each tree, while Drozdan was carefully listening and nodding in approval. Or at least, that was how it looked, as I was not paying attention to this lecture, not even for a second.
I surrendered all my attention to the beauty that was surrounding us.

My eyes couldn't handle the vividly saturated colors that were embracing me in a bear hug. It looked like a mad artist had been commissioned to paint the area, but has had a nervous breakdown mid-way... ferociously throwing his paint palette across the landscape. Every shade of green, brown and yellow imaginable were swept around in this tornado of color that had overwhelmed the region... a visual masterpiece that was inconceivable... unless you saw it in person.

The soil beneath our feet was cold and a bit moist. The ground was covered with leaves, twigs, parts of plants, grass and a few lady bugs and ants scattered here and there, going about their daily business.

Marko carried a big hand-made hemp knapsack, that was loaded with a few sandwiches, a bottle of water and three containers for the berries. Drozdan also carried a backpack, but I was too afraid to ask him what was inside.

Since we entered the woods, he hadn't spoken to me that much. I was hoping to keep it that way.

We moved expeditiously along the main pathway, entering the deeper part of the woods, where the terrain was uneven, and little hills and slopes had started to appear from nowhere.

"Mother nature rewards us with her fruit!" Drozdan exclaimed as he was pointing to a little strawberry bush.

"Are you sure these are strawberries?" I asked, squatting and picking a fruit up, then analyzing it with suspicious eyes. "This looks really small compared to the strawberries in the garden!" I concluded.

"This tiny ball of magic will blow you away, my brother…" the happy monk said, looking me straight in the eyes.

"Ok, you're freaking me out now, Drozdan!" I replied with a scared look on my face.

"Just give it a try…you will not regret it…you know!" he said while picking up a small fruit himself and throwing it in his mouth, without even washing it first.

"You didn't even wash the fruit?!" I was surprised.

"Mother nature wants you to experience her in all her natural glory and beauty," Drozdan replied.

"I don't know where you are going with this…and you're talking about it in an oddly sexual way," I mumbled, as this man was once again knocking down all my rational thoughts and concepts about life. "If I eat the strawberry without washing it, will you please stop being weird…even if it's for a few minutes?" I tried to negotiate with him.

"Deal!" he resounded.

I quickly threw the little piece of crimson red fruit in my mouth. A few snappy chews later and… boom! My taste buds were under attack; a concentrated explosion, closely followed by an intense assault of flavor!

My eyes widened and my mind started racing.

"Wow, this is unbelievable! So much sweetness in something so small!" I exclaimed, while looking at the bush with the berries on. "I feel different…in a good way," I finished, while looking at Drozdan.

"Nice…right?" the happy monk stated in a calm voice. "I come to the forest and eat wild fruit once a week. They really help me to open up my middle chakra," he explained as he and Marko started to pick the berries from the bush.

"Open your what? Oh no…please don't tell me these are some sort of weird hallucinogenic wild berries, and I will go crazy in an hour?!" I said with a worried look on my face.

Drozdan turned his head away from the strawberry picking and said, "I don't know…but I eat from here, and I'm absolutely normal."

"I'm dead…" I said, exhaling and looking at the bush.

A minute later, the plant was left completely naked and stripped of its yield. Even though the fruits were many, their individual size was miniature, so they barely covered the bottom of the containers. We obviously needed much more!

The terrain started to mimic a roller coaster ride, as there were lots of rock and soil formations going up and down. Along the way, we reached a pathway that had two little hilly slopes on each side.

"Oh…I see something!" Drozdan announced in a loud voice. "I'll be right back!"

He took a few steps and slid down the grassy slope. Kalina's father and I used that little pause in our trip as an opportunity to drink some water. As the old man was getting out the bottle of liquid, I tried to break the awkward silence.

"So...do you come to the woods?" I asked him, right before I took a sip. "Probably often… to get away from the wife…right?" I finished, after a refreshing drink.

He didn't understand a single word, and gave me a mean look instead. As I passed the bottle back to him, I was determined to land my silly wisecrack.

"If you don't understand my words, you will understand my re-enactment!" I said, preparing to physically demonstrate and play out my joke. "You, Marko," I pointed at him, speaking loudly and slowly, "come to the woods," I continued, mimicking a person walking, using my index and middle finger, and then pointing to the trees, "to get away," I started running in one place, "from Ginka," I said, pretending to talk with my left hand.

Marko puzzled over the pantomime, and after this brief session of charades, he understood the joke! He erupted with laughter!

"Yes, you got it!" I yelled with a huge smile on my face.

He was definitely amused, giving me a reassuring thumbs up.

"Ah…nothing like a good old dash of sexism in the evening!" I said very sarcastically, while deeply inhaling the fresh air and looking around.

"ARRGGHHHH…YOU LITTLE SHIT!!" a loud scream slashed through the calm atmosphere.

I instantly recognized the voice and the location it was coming from, so I made my way to the small slope on the left of the pathway we were on.

"Drozdan! What happened? Are you ok?" I asked, looking down on him from the top of the slope. "Why is there a hedgehog next to you?" I questioned with a bewildered expression on my face.

"I found him on the ground…it's a gift from mother nature, brother," the happy monk said, while holding his hand.

"Ok…sure…so what happened?" I asked.

"I picked him up…and I wanted to give him a hug, and to tell him that he's a creation of the universe, you know?" he said, looking up at me.

"Of course…as you do with a hedgehog," I said very sarcastically.

"Yes, exactly! I started to whisper a powerful cleansing mantra for his middle chakra, so he could be as enlightened as me," he explained.

"I don't see anything wrong, to be honest…you're doing the Lord's work over there," I replied, barely keeping a straight face.

"Yes! Thank you! That's what I said to the hedgehog after he lashed out at me so viciously!"

As Drozdan was walking back up to the pathway, I asked him, "So, how did he attack you?"

"Well, as I started to chant my mantra to him, I saw the enlightenment coming to life in his eyes, you know… so I wanted to transmit some energy, and I gave him a big hug, but he pricked me with his sharp spines and bit me on the nose!" he exclaimed.

"He bit you on the nose?!" I was vibrating with the laughter that I was trying to keep inside me.

When he came nearer, I could see a few marks on his nose from the bite and the redness all over his forearms where the hedgehog had pricked him. I felt really sorry for him. Even though he is really bizarre, I think his heart is in the right place; he doesn't mean harm to anybody or anything.

I put my arm around him in an attempt to comfort him, as he looked distressed.

"You will be fine, buddy…and for future reference, wild animals don't really appreciate chakra cleansing and mantra singing," I told him, while trying to remain serious.

"They don't?!" The happy monk was in shock.

"No, they don't…especially bears! Never try to cleanse the chakra of a bear!" I said, looking him in the eyes.

"Thank you for the advice, James…you are a good friend!" he said as he gave me a pat on the back and a big sincere smile.

A quick thought surfaced in my mind. "He called me a friend! That is something people don't refer to me as very often."

In the meantime, Marko had been observing the aftermath of Drozdan's encounter with the hedgehog and me comforting him, shaking his head in disbelief, and managing to give us just the beginning of a smile.

We bravely carried on with our quest to find as much sweet fruit for the jam that the girls were about to prepare. We continued walking along the main pathway, and as we entered a deeper part of the woods, a few bushes of red and dark blue fruit appeared nearby. We stopped and picked everything that was in sight; the two containers were half full by this point. We were doing well as the sun started its slow descent and the day was trying to turn into night.

The old man was looking at his wristwatch and talking to Drozdan.

"Is everything ok?" I asked the happy monk.

"James…it will be dark soon, so we will need to speed up and collect as much fruit from mother nature as we can, then we need to go."

"I'm not in a hurry, don't worry. I'm really starting to like this place, you know…the nature is so beautiful and so welcoming!" I said, while sitting down on the top of a huge rock covered in grass and mushrooms.

"Bears and wolves…if we stay, I will have to cleanse their chakras in person, my brother…they need some spiritual guidance," Drozdan was rambling again.

"Hold on!" I stood up and raised both my hands. "Repeat the beginning of that sentence!" I commanded the happy monk.

"Bears and wolves," he repeated.

"There are bears and wolves in this forest?!!!" I screamed in panic. "Give me this bucket!" I snatched Drozdan's container from his hand. "Here berry, berry…Berries come out and play!" I had completely lost my mind.

I was whistling and walking around frantically, calling the green-red bushes to appear from nowhere. I detected one, and I quickly ran over and squatted next to it, then started picking the small fruits at a rapid pace.

"So, the quicker we fill these damn buckets…the quicker we can go home, and not get eaten by wild animals…right?" I asked, while swiftly collecting sweet fruit and hyperventilating at the same time.

"Yes, brother…but the animals in this forest are kind souls. I speak with them…they have fascinating stories, you know," Drozdan was verbally garbling again.

"Of course you do, you lunatic!" I mumbled really quietly to myself.

My stress was boiling over, and my anxieties and fears were raging all through my body now.

"Ok, this bush is done," I said, as I had filled up half of the container with strawberries. "Let's go guys...I see more bushes up ahead!" I declared, marching forward...

We really picked up the tempo at this point. Time started to sprint, and night was coming very quickly. Half an hour later, we were all done; three small containers were jam packed with fruit!

"Mission complete!" I yelled and gave a high five to both guys. "Now let's get the hell out of here, before the wolves and bears turn us into mincemeat!"

Twenty minutes later, we were out of the woods. Marko knew the territory like the back of his hand, and with a trusty flashlight in his right palm, it was an easy escape, with no wild animals trying to eat us... always a positive outcome!

We passed that little timber house right at the beginning of the woods, then clambered over the small hill and across the improvised bridge constructed with thick ropes and plywood.

"Ah...I can see the house from here!" I exhaled all of a sudden and looked at Drozdan.

"Did you enjoy this journey...my brother?" he replied.

"You know what...I actually did! It had its ups and downs, but overall, thank you for the experience!" I said, smiling politely.

"What part did you enjoy the most?" the happy monk asked me.

"Hearing you cursing a hedgehog; that was pretty funny!" I said as I tapped him on the shoulder and started laughing.

Before I knew it, we were in front of the house. Drozdan handed over the little bucket that he had been carrying and waved goodbye, then went home.

I was feeling full of pride and joy, believing that I had contributed, and I was ready to display our gatherings in front of my wife.

We walked upstairs. I opened the front door and yelled, "Honey, I'm home! And guess what we've gathered for you!"

"We're in the kitchen upstairs!" her voice came from above.

I joined her and Ginka as they were talking and cooking.

"Here are the berries you girls wanted!" I gave them the three small containers full of red and blue fruit.

I was so full of delight and excitement, as the journey into the woods had not been easy for me. At this point, I was dirty, really exhausted and mentally drained from all of Drozdan's nonsense, but it was worth it, as I'd completed the quest and provided the berries for my wife.

"Oh…thank you! Where are the rest?" Kalina asked as she took the little buckets.

"What do you mean, the rest? That's all of them!" I replied.

Kalina turned to her mother and swiftly translated our conversation. They both started laughing.

"Oh dear…there is no way that this will be enough…there are going to be around three thousand people at the festival!" she said.

"Three thousand people! You have to feed them all?!" I fired back.

"Oh c'mon, don't be silly," she was laughing. "We need three times the amount you gathered today," she concluded.

Ginka started talking with Kalina and pointing to the fruit.

"Oh, it turns out that there is a strawberry and blueberry salesman at the end of the village…My mother will go tomorrow and get some more for the jam," Kalina explained while putting both hands on her hips. "Well…it turns out, you didn't need to go into the woods after all!" She started laughing again.

I was so tired that I couldn't even get mad.

"I'll take a shower, eat something and go straight to bed," I exhaled.

"Ok dear…we will serve dinner in a bit," my wife said.

After a quick wash, I devoured my dinner downstairs. I was so worn out from the adventure in the woods that I didn't have the energy to analyze and describe what I was consuming or what was happening around me. Heck, I couldn't even remember what I had for supper!

After I'd finished the food, I said goodnight to everyone. In no time, I changed into my pajamas, carried out my nightly routine, then crashed into one of the softest and most comfortable beds I'd ever had the pleasure to sleep in. I dozed off immediately.

## 07.24.1985 (Wednesday)

"COCK-A-DOODLE-DOO!!!"
"COCK-A-DOODLE-DOO!!!"
"COCK-A-DOODLE-DOO!!!"
"Ah…not again!" I muttered incredulously as I put the pillow over my face.
"COCK-A-DOODLE-DOO!!!"
"COCK-A-DOODLE-DOO!!!"
"COCK-A-DOODLE-DOO!!!"
"Why the hell is the sound coming from two different directions? Does this crazy bird have a speaker installed across the village?" I said, half asleep.

I slowly raised myself, planted my feet on the ground and sat on the side of the bed, looking and feeling like shit! Eventually, I put my slippers on and managed to drag myself to the sink in the little kitchen for a cup of water. As I was refreshing myself, I saw our rooster singing his heart out from the window again, but right after he finished his set, another tenor fired back at him this time.

"Hold on, what's happening?!" I grunted. "Are there two roosters now?"

I took my glass with me and went to the little terrace that was adjacent to the room, overlooking Drozdan's house. I saw that the window right next to his front door was wide open, and the happy monk's pet rooster Gagarin was standing on top of the windowsill, hollering at our rooster.

"Oh God, are they having a crowing competition now…?" I exhaled while looking down and holding my forehead. "I just can't catch a break in this crazy place…or a moment of peace and quiet," I mumbled, while walking back into the room. "Ok James…you can't fall asleep again with all this racket…Be an adult and drag yourself to the guest room and have breakfast with the family," I instructed myself.

Somehow, I managed to haul my body to the main area where all the activity was happening. I opened the door, and the same scenario as the day before greeted me; everyone was having a morning meal, and the TV was blasting like crazy.

"Can we…turn the volume down…please?!" I shouted, miming at the same time.

"What?!" Kalina yelled.

"Never mind…" I limped my way over to the TV and turned the volume down myself. "Morning everybody!" I chimed as I sat down.

"Somebody had a good night's sleep!" my spouse said, while passing me the jar with the delicious red pesto inside and a few pieces of bread.

I wolfed down my breakfast, and then wanted to hide in one of the many rooms that this house had to offer. I was feeling tired and just couldn't be bothered to do anything all day.

"Oh…that was great, dear! Thank you for the food…I'm going to go and relax on a couch somewhere in this house," I said to Kalina, while slowly getting up from the table.

"Well…the guests will be here in two hours…I think you should change out of your pajamas and get ready," she said.

"The guests!?" I exclaimed. "What guests?!" I was not thrilled by this prospect.

"It's midweek, so that means that people go to each other's houses for coffee, tea, sweets and gossip," my wife explained, seeming very happy.

"How many people are coming?"

"Around twenty," she casually threw the number around the room.

"Twenty?!" My anxieties started to riot inside me. "Do I have to participate in this?" I asked, hoping she would say no.

"Yes!" she insisted.

"Damn it!" I muttered.

"Don't worry, it will be fine! You will have fun, I promise," my love tried to calm me down.

The minutes were rushing by as I washed my face and changed into something a bit more presentable. After some time, I returned to the main guest room, where the girls had worked their magic and had prepared a welcome feast of snacks worthy of royalty.

Before I knew it, the time had come! It was around 11am, and the guests were about to arrive any minute. My stomach was in a ball, my palms were sweaty, and I felt light-headed. I was pacing back and forth around the two big tables, which were covered with all sorts of sweets, treats, fizzy drinks, tea and coffee pods, whilst having a nervous breakdown.

I heard noises coming from outside and quickly rushed over to the big window that was almost the size of the wall, drawing back the thin transparent curtain that was trying to cover it.

Right across the street, I saw the guests; there were around twenty people, but it seemed like an army platoon was coming to finish me off.

A few minutes later, the doorbell rang several times. I quickly joined the rest of the family, who were in the corridor, a few moments away from meeting the invaders.

Ginka opened the front door, and there they were…an army of glowing faces…a horde of buzzing energy…one by one taking the stairs and storming the house.

Hugs, kisses on cheeks, laughter and positivity were flying everywhere, bouncing off the walls… They didn't spare me, as I fell victim to that contagious affection these people were accustomed to show.

The volume of chatter was loud and unfathomable to me. We slowly made our way to the main room, where the ceremony of gossip, coffee and tea drinking was about to take place.

A few minutes later, everyone was seated, except Kalina and her mother, who were maneuvering near the tables with big jugs of java and tea, and giving out cookies and sweets.

Somehow, they had managed to convince or force Marko to stay, at least for the time being. He didn't look so happy about the whole situation that was occurring, as the crowd was mostly made up of old women with a few young grandchildren and two disgruntled old men, who looked like they'd lost a serious bet with their wives and had been dragged here.

As I was quietly eating a cookie in the corner and drinking some soothing tea, I observed the absurdity that was unfolding in front of my eyes. Vessels of verbal mishmash were dumped in the area, and I was not sure what they were talking about… Were they discussing the latest advances in the field of astrophysics, or perhaps debating the geo-economics of the village? In all fairness, it looked like they were gossiping about who slept with whom in the latest episode of the telenovela that was radiating from the TV.

All the women's voices were very high pitched. The sounds were all blending together, and since I didn't understand what they were saying, it all sounded like gibberish, allowing me to easily zone out… At one point, it started to sound like clucking, and they all sounded like chickens!

I turned to Marko, who was involuntarily sitting next to me, at the area of the table that was unofficially marked as the "man corner." I tapped him with my elbow and turned my palm in to a little chicken's beak. As he looked at me, I started making some hen noises in a quiet voice.

"They all sound like that right now!" I said, while giving a Broadway-worthy performance.

He started laughing. The lingo of pantomime and misogyny is international, and not even a language barrier could stop it. I don't know why, but sexism was a quick way to get Kalina's father to laugh. However, I was just joking around, as the women in this village were some truly bad-ass females, working alongside the men in the farms, mines and factories, whilst raising children, looking after the house and their husbands, enjoying a happy and fulfilling social life and having close friendships.

The hours were dragging by, and at this point in the whole weird experience, I was getting very bored, as nothing was happening, and I didn't understand a word of the verbal hurricane that was thrashing around the room.

Marko stood up, went over to Ginka, said something, then went out.

"Ah… he saved himself!" I thought. "I wonder what he said to her? How did he manage to flee this madness?"

As I was coming up with a plan of escape in my mind, everyone went quiet all of a sudden. The three little children that were a part of this cluster of people stood up and made their way to the front of the TV, so they were in clear view of everyone.

I had no idea what was happening right then, as the three young kids were standing in front of everyone and…one boy started to recite what I could only imagine was some sort of a poem.

After about thirty seconds, the youngster took a bow, and everyone started clapping. Then another poor little soul started reciting a similar poem or a song or a cooking recipe… I had no idea what was happening.

As Kalina was at the other end of the table, and a ton of people were between us, I didn't have my trusted guide to translate and help me out, so, I was left on my own to decode this mystery.

Suddenly, the last child started singing, and the other two began hopping around like rabbits… it was getting deeply weird now. I had no idea what to do with my hands and face… Did I have to applaud this madness, or simply nod and smile in approval, like the rest of the people?

I felt like a Roman emperor watching the gladiators fight to the death. Was I supposed to give them a thumbs up or thumbs down and decide their fate?

I needed to get out, as this entertainment or competition… whatever the hell it was… was getting out of hand. At this point, the little kids were recreating some sort of theatrical play. I stood up and walked around the table to find Kalina at the other end, near the fireplace.

"Hey…honey, I don't feel so well…I think I ate too many cookies," I said to my wife. "I'm going to go upstairs and lay down for a bit, ok?" I was lying my face off.

"Oh…is everything ok? Yes, of course, get some rest. Do you want me to make you some tea?" She seemed genuinely concerned about me.

"I'm fine, I just need a bit of rest," I said and left as quickly as I could.

As I closed the door from the outside, I whispered, "Sweet…freedom! Ok, James, a cocktail and a view of the mountains… that's what you need right now!" I exclaimed and made my way to the little guest room where I was staying.

Cabinet… fridge… kitchen! The routine was tattooed on my brain. I kidnapped the innocent bottles of gin and tonic from the cabinet, elected a glass from the kitchen, in which I sacrificed a few ice cubes that bumped heads at the bottom, dropped a few atomic slices of lemon and lime, drowned everything in booze, and planted a proud red straw!

"Ah…look at that…perfection!" I announced, raising my newly created work of art. "I need to find a peaceful place. I know…the big terrace next to the storage room upstairs."

I swiftly made my way up there. Before I knew it, I was out on the spacious terrace, with two camping chairs and a small plastic table… excellent!

"Ah…this is heaven," I said as I dropped my exhausted body onto one of the chairs. "A drink in my hand…and the view of a lifetime!" I finally took a long sip from my favorite drink!

The terrace was overlooking the forests and the mountains, that were impossible to visually escape. I was falling in love with this scenery. Since I'd arrived, with every hour that passed, I was appreciating this captivating topography more and more.

When I was a kid, I remember exploring nature every summer. I had a fascination with animals and the environment. But when you get older, things change, life changes… Back home, I am stuck in a cubicle, working in a big soulless building. I know that the titles of journalist and writer are prestigious, but sometimes I feel…

"Crack… crack… crack… crack!" A noise was coming from inside the room.

"What the hell!" I said as I stood up from the chair. "Oh… Marko… you scared me!" I exclaimed with relief in my voice, as Kalina's father crossed the room and stood at the door to the terrace. "Ugh… have a seat… please join me!" I said as I extended my hand and pointed to the empty chair near me.

He raised his hand, said something and disappeared quickly.

"I don't know what's happening right now…and I'm too tired to even care," I exhaled, then took a refreshing sip of my drink.

No more than thirty seconds later, Marko walked onto the balcony again, this time holding a crystal glass and a small bottle of gold-ish liquid, which had an appealing and mysterious rusty glow.

"Ah…you went for the alcohol…I see," I said with a big smile on my face, followed by a little chuckle.

A few moments later, his glass was full. We both raised our crystals, and I said, "Cheers!" The glasses collided and created a pleasant clinking sound.

We were both looking at the surrounding nature and admiring it. It was peaceful and quiet. No words were spoken between us. It was like a meditation session, accompanied by booze and trees.

All of a sudden, Kalina's father stood up and went inside.

"Did I do something to offend him?" I thought out loud.

A minute passed, and he was still inside. I started to worry, so I stood up and went into the room.

"Marko?!" I called, while looking around.

Noises were coming from the little private area, which I had only taken a peek in during the guided house tour and had never fully stepped inside.

"Marko…are you in there?" I said as I knocked on the door, which was ajar. "Hey… here you are! I was worrying about you!" I said, even though I knew not a single word would be understood by him.

He was digging through the many boxes that were scattered all around the room, pulling random objects from each one. When he saw me, he constructed half a smile, put a bunch of little things in a medium-sized box and stomped off to the terrace once again.

"What the hell is happening here?" I said as I followed the old man back to the balcony.

We sat down, and I took a sip of my delicious creation. The glass was half empty at this point. Marko started pulling out little red and green cases with smooth edges, relatively small in size, all with nice matte finishes and decorated with embroidery on top.

"Oh…what is this? Looks interesting!" I said as Marko was still getting stuff out of the box.

The old man opened a few of the cases. Inside were medals.

"Oh wow…these are yours?" I asked, lifting my eyes from the shiny, delicately sculpted awards. "Medal for bravery!"

I was mesmerized by the reflection and the status that these little commemorative antiques possessed. This man was a military hero and a veteran!

He started showing me pictures of when he was a teenager in the military, and then working in the mines, followed by wedding pictures of him and Ginka, and Kalina as a baby. He was looking at the prints, one after the other, and talking whilst taking tiny sips from his drink. His eyes filled up with tears.

I was surprised and a bit shocked at the sight of this burly man becoming tearful over pictures and talking to them. I thought the alcohol had got to him as he refilled his glass.

He looked at me, cracked a tiny smile and nodded a few times. After searching for something on the table, he slid a red box containing a medal towards me, making a gesture that translated to, "It's for you!"

"Oh, no… no, I can't except that!" I said as I slid the prestigious award back to him.

He took the acknowledgement of bravery in his hand and stood up, took a step or two, leaned over and gave me the medal. I felt awkward, so I had no choice but to accept it.

Marko was visibly happy at the fact that I'd accepted his offering. He went back to his seat, pounded his fist on the table and said something in his language. He seemed ecstatic.

"Cheers!" he said in broken English.

"Hey…yes, cheers!" I erupted as I raised my crystal again and gave his glass another clink.

We spent some time looking at the naturally pleasing features of the surrounding area and taking sips of our drinks, which were almost finished.

"James…James…where are you, dear?" the voice of my love called.

"I'm on the terrace, honey!" I yelled back.

"Hey…there you are!" she said with a big smile on her face as she walked onto the balcony. "You guys having fun?"

"Hey…yes, we are enjoying the view of the mountains, and your father was showing me some of his old medals and pictures," I answered.

Marko started talking to Kalina, taking a sip of his almost-finished drink. He took a look at me, and then slapped the table.

"Oh!" my wife looked at me and said, "My dad is going to see his friends from his mining days. They will be having some food and drinks…He insists that you join him!" she translated.

"Oh…where is this?" I asked with surprise in my voice.

"When you went to the woods to pick berries yesterday… did you see a wooden shack at the beginning of the forest?" she asked me.

"Yes!" I said.

"Well, there, in that cabin!" she replied.

"There…in the woods…in the dark…drinking?!" I asked, not sure that partying in an area filled with wolves and bears was such a good idea.

"Yes…it will be fun! My dad is starting to warm up to you…and it will be an insult to him if you don't go along," she explained. "You will probably have some appetizers and drink a glass or two of wine, that's it. I don't think it will take that long," she said.

"Ok…if it's important to you, it's important to me," I smiled as I stood up from my chair.

Kalina translated to her father that I would go with him and he slapped both his palms together and said something out loud.

"You are going in ten minutes, dear!" she said.

"Oh, ok, I'm going downstairs to change quickly, then I will be in front of the house waiting for him. Oh…can you ask him why he gave me this?" I said as I showed her the medal.

"He gave you his bravery medal?!" Kalina was surprised. "Ok, I'll ask him and will tell you later."

"Ok, great!" I said as I put the medal in my pocket, waved goodbye to my wife and headed downstairs to change.

I took out the precious new gift that Marko had given me and put it in the right pocket of my other jeans, just for safe keeping.

No more than ten minutes later, I was all ready and waiting in front of the house. The old man showed up, wearing his casual working clothes. I was wearing a nice button-down checked shirt with blue jeans and sneakers.

The old man led the way, as we headed along a now familiar route. We passed Drozdan's brick house, then walked down the dirt pathway.

A few minute later, we were at the riverside, then we passed over the unstable bridge. After a few more minutes of walking, we saw the wooden shack at the edge of the forest.

It was already getting dark, and I could barely see anything, but the cabin was filled with light, which was shining brightly in the distance.

We finally arrived, and after a couple of solid knocks, the front door slowly opened. We were greeted by a surge of foreign sounds, which flooded the whole area.

At the door was a man the size of a brown bear walking on two feet!

A firm handshake followed by a shoulder hug was exchanged between this giant and Marko.

The man looked like an off-duty lumberjack… bushy beard, broad shoulders, plaid pattern shirt, jeans and work boots. He extended a palm and barked out his name.

"Drago!" he said to me, and before I knew it, he had crushed my hand.

"Ugh… James… nice to meet you!" I squealed, visibly in pain.

We were invited inside. A few steps in, and I was in the middle of utter chaos and madness… the party was in full swing!

These were all of Marko's old buddies from his mining days; all in their late 50s, early 60s… built like tanks… all of them wearing t-shirts, even though it was freezing outside.

The wooden cabin was not that big; it seemed like it was one main room, with a bedroom, small kitchen and a bathroom. As I quickly scanned the structure, I confirmed my assumption. The fact that all the doors to the rooms were slightly opened also helped a lot with my hypothesis.

The main area was almost identical to the big guest space back in Kalina's house, with the only difference being that, in this room there were three half-drunk, sturdy men, singing, waving their hands around and shouting at each other.

A firm slap on the shoulder interrupted my inner dialog I saw the host of the evening smiling at me, and with a thick voice, he said something in his own language.

There was no one to translate or help me out here…I was in a linguistic wasteland…I smiled back politely.

Drago raised his hand in an inviting manner and pointed to one of the seats that was available; a space on a padded bench, similar to the one in Marko's house.

I took a seat and looked around. Heavy inferno balls shooting from the fireplace were raising the temperature of the room intensely. I eyeballed the table to see what type of offering the host had presented. There were mostly variations of salami, olives, pickles and goat cheese… and a few big bottles of that gold-ish liquid I saw in the cabinet back in the house.

"Uh-oh, this is not going to be a sociable event where we discuss poetry, art and culture… This is going to be a heavy drinking and let's hope we don't get eaten by bears in the woods event!" I nervously said to myself.

Everyone had a crystal in front of them. A wave of "Cheers!" erupted, as everyone looked to me and my empty glass…

"Do you have gin and tonic?" I screamed over the music, which was shaking the foundations of the building.

"GIN?!" Drago shouted followed by loud, thunderous laughter.

He started talking in his language, while looking at me… proudly lifting the home-made alcoholic drink… "GIN?!…NO!" he yelled "This…*RAKIQ*," he said, pointing at the gold-colored bottle… "THE BEST!" he was screaming and giving a thumbs up.

He resembled a tipsy lumberjack who had recently got sacked from the logging industry and had fallen on hard times, so to make ends meet, he was peddling bottles of booze, door to door with his magnificent sales pitch, "This…*RAKIQ*…THE BEST!"

I didn't want to be rude or to seem snobbish, so I said, "Ah… what's the worst that can happen? Pour me some *Rakiq*!" I raised my empty glass and shot a thumbs up back at him.

He slowly poured the liquid gold, which gently trickled and filled up my crystal.

"SALUTE!" everyone yelled… Our glasses bashed together, then I took a serious sip of this mysterious liquid.

"God Almighty!" I screamed. "It burns!"

This drink was the strongest alcohol I'd ever tried in my life… it felt like a punch to the throat!

I started to burn up instantly… and the thick, long-sleeved, button-down shirt I was wearing didn't help. Drago pointed at the shirt, lifted his shoulders and wobbled his head. I translated that as, "What do you call this in your language?"

"Oh, you mean this?" I pointed at the piece of clothing. "SHIRT!" I yelled back.

"Shirt?!" the host repeated. He gave me an approving thumbs up, and we both took a big sip of our drinks.

The radio was blasting eccentric sounds, the roaring fireplace was heating up the atmosphere, and the other two people, who I hadn't even been introduced to, were drinking, laughing and eating pickles. This was a chaotic atmosphere, as the alcohol was strong, and I was a weak drinker…

I took my shirt off, as the heat was unbearable…"Fuck it!" I yelled and pointed at Drago. "This bravery juice is not that bad!" I said and took another manly sip. "Give me some more *RAKIQ*!" I screamed as the alcohol was definitely kicking in by this point, and the music had started to sound better and better with each passing minute.

Seconds later, and with the kindness of the host, my glass was full again.

I stood up and shouted, "Ok…let's drink to family, friendship and bears in the woods! Salute!" I yelled, and everyone raised their glasses.

They all guzzled down their drinks in a single swig, and I started to pour the heavily concentrated booze into my mouth.

"SHIRT! SHIRT! SHIRT! SHIRT!" Everyone was chanting and stomping their feet as I was trying to finish off the contents of the small glass. It felt like a frat party, and everyone wanted me to chug the firewater.

"HA!…It's funny you know…Hiccup!…Because, you know…. Hahaha!" I was slurring my speech heavily, but my body was buzzing with energy. I tried to finish my sentence. "You think I'm shirt? Oh, wait, you think my name is shirt! HA!"

I stumbled to the corner and picked up my piece of clothing that I'd unceremoniously tossed onto the ground.

"No, this not me!" I was pointing at my flannel shirt that I had previously been wearing. "This is Larry…" Why I said that, I had no idea! I'd never given a name to an inanimate object before. "But I… James, you know…" My head was starting to spin, or was it the room that was spinning…I was not sure. "Ah… who cares! I'M SHIRT! I'M SHIRT!" I was yelling and everyone was laughing and drinking.

They started pounding on the table yelling, "I'M SHIRT! I'M SHIRT! I'M SHIRT!"

"Ok…I think I need a refill…Bartender!" I screeched and pointed at Drago. "*RAKIQ*!" I raised my crystal as high as I could and vocalized my wish in the most enthusiastic way.

Smiles and laughter ware ricocheting off the walls, the heat started to feel very comfortable, the music had a certain charming rhythm to it that I started to like, and I loved everyone in the room with all my heart…yup…I was very drunk!

Oh, what a picture to witness; my newly-named button-down shirt Larry in one hand and a glass of *Rakiq* in the other; a spirit so strong that it could melt your face off.

I decided to attempt something that should be illegal in all fifty states and many countries around the world. James Elmswood attempted to dance!

"This is my song!" I barely managed to get the sentence out of my mouth.

I pointed to the powerful sound system and gave it a thumbs up. Drago stood up and turned the volume up. I was in front of the table, on the little makeshift dance floor. I started to move in different directions, flapping my arms all over the place, my coordination and dancing skills non-existent.

The music sounded so powerful and seemed to have an emotional effect on the rest of the men, as they all jumped up and hugged each other over the arms and started moving in a synchronized manner, from side to side…

Everyone was singing unbelievably loud, while alcohol was spilling out of the glasses that the men were still holding on to. The songs kept going and going. I lost track of time. I had no idea what was happening. I didn't even know which planet we were on anymore. My world was spinning…

We sat down on the table. The booze didn't stop. The singing got louder with every shot of *Rakiq*, followed by a piece of pickle, pounding on the table and screaming… We did this over and over and over… until I completely blacked out…

# 07.25.1985 (Thursday)

I was awoken in a fashion that unfortunately I was becoming accustomed to by this point. The rooster was telling me that it was time to rise and shine. After a few minutes, I finally managed to open my eyes and mumbled in a raspy voice, "Argh…my head…it's killing me!"

It felt like somebody had hit me with a potato sack full of bricks.

"God damn it…why does it hurt so much!?"

The pain was intense, and I didn't have the energy or the will to drag myself to the window to tell the rooster to piss off. I just laid in bed, half dead, listening to that crazy little animal.

"Well, that's it, James…you will die now…nobody will find you!" I was miserably mumbling to myself as I was falling in and out of sleep.

"James…are you ok, honey?" a suiting voice was dancing around the room.

I opened my eyes and saw my savior…Kalina.

"This is the end for me, my love." I reached out with my hand, as she came closer, sitting at the end of the bed.

"Oh dear, did you get really drunk last night?" she asked.

"I remember what happened only up to a certain point…I'm afraid for your father. He drank a lot," I muttered. "For a man his age, he is probably in the hospital right now?!"

"Hospital?" Kalina laughed. "He is outside, shirtless, plowing the field."

"You people are crazy!" I barely had the strength to speak.

"You need to be careful with *Rakiq* hangovers, you know," she explained. "*Rakiq* has around 50% alcohol in it, and you drank home-made stuff… that is so powerful, it will take you into outer space," she laughed hysterically.

"I think I'm on Pluto right now," I said.

"Well, you'd better get back to Earth soon, because we are going to the big festival today," she said.

"Oh…can I stay in bed, please?" I pleaded.

"No, we really need your help!" she said. "You know what…I will help you defeat that headache and hangover…just a moment," Kalina offered, springing into action and leaving the room to look for something.

A few moments later, she walked in with a big jar of pickles and a plate. Removing all the green veg from the jar and putting them on the dish, she handed me over a massive jug of dark green juice.

"Drink!" she ordered.

"What?!" I knitted my eyebrows into a frown. "This is pickle juice! You're not supposed to drink that!"

"If you want to get better fast, drink the whole jar…If you want to be in agony, don't do anything and stay in bed," she emphasized.

She had a point, as I was desperate to get rid of that hangover and the excruciating pain trapped in my body.

"Here goes nothing!" I said as I raised myself and sat on the side of the bed, taking a serious gulp. "Damn, this thing is so bitter and salty!" I screamed as the pickled liquid was sloshing around in my mouth. "Wow, this is intense!" my face crumpled.

After a minute of serious hangover-juice drinking, the big jar was empty.

"How do you feel?" Kalina looked at me inquisitively.

"A bit better actually," I answered in surprise.

"Good…time for phase two!" she said.

"What?! Phase two? What are you talking about?" I was not excited.

"Come to the table, dear… I'll be back in 10 minutes. I think we have some," my wife said and left the room.

I managed to drag my half-dead body to the chair and lay my arms and head on the dining table.

Sometime later, the door opened, and my wife walked in with a tray.

"Here you go, dear…my secret weapon!" she offered as she put the platter on the table and explained what I was looking at. "Pig belly soup!" She pointed to a full bowl. "In order to make it work, you need to add the extra ingredients…vinegar, garlic, and chili peppers."

"Hold on, what?!" I spoke up. "Pork belly? Add vinegar and garlic? This doesn't sound right!"

"Trust me…this will make you feel great, and it's delicious!" she insisted.

A few moments later, the correct dosage of all the extra elements had been added to the hot soup, and a piece of white fluffy bread was casually resting on the tray as well.

"Eat this…You will feel better!" she said.

We were talking while I was slowly eating. The soup was surprisingly delicious; an unusual taste, I might add, as the mixture of ingredients didn't make much sense to me, but I did enjoy it.

"Ok, so, we need to leave for the festival at 12 o'clock. Take this aspirin and go to bed for a few more hours. You will feel like new!" She handed over the little white tablet and a glass of water.

I took the medicine and looked at the time. It was 7:30am, and I needed to get up at 11am.

"I will come and wake you up if you're still sleeping," Kalina said and left the room.

I was feeling much better, but still tired from the wild party the previous night. I dragged myself back into bed and fell asleep quickly.

I woke up around the time I was supposed to.

"Oh my God! I feel good now!" I was surprised.

I took a quick shower and changed into something more comfortable.

A few moments later, I located the rest of the family in the living room upstairs that had a tiny kitchen attached to it, as they were preparing the final touches for the big festival.

"Hey… morning everyone!" I said with a glowing expression.

"Morning!" my wife replied, and her parents waved at me as I entered the room.

"Are you better now?" Kalina asked.

"I feel like a new man!" I was joyful.

"Well Mr. New Man…my father was just telling us what shenanigans you got up to last night at their little party!" she teased, while polishing small jars filled with homemade jam and placing them very carefully in a case.

"Oh…well, I do remember a few things," I raised my eyebrows.

"How is your friend Larry the shirt?" She seemed jolly.

"Oh my God…what was I up to?!" I said, shaking my head in disbelief.

"Your dancing skills are impressive…or so I was told!"
she continued. "But your handling of alcohol, not so
much!"

Everyone was laughing at this point, as both her
parents knew what she was talking about.

"Well, this booze was so strong…it knocked me out!" I
started laughing as well.

"We are almost ready to go, dear!" Kalina said as she
placed the last jar in the final case.

"Do you need any help?" I asked.

"We actually do. If you can help my father to bring
everything downstairs in front of the house, that would be
excellent!"

I jumped up and started carrying the not-so-heavy
plastic cases filled with small jars of homemade jam and
boxes packed with all sorts of treats and sweets.

After fifteen minutes or so, everything was piled up in
front of the house.

"How are we going to carry all these things to the
festival?" I asked, pointing to the thick cardboard boxes
and plastic cases.

"My father will bring out trolleys. It will be easy!"
Kalina smiled.

Marko mysteriously pulled out three carts, which were
made of heavy-duty steel, low to the ground and with a
large storage capacity. A few minutes later, everything
was tidily packed, and we were ready to go.

"Off we go!" my wife exclaimed, and we started
walking.

"Where is this festival taking place? Is it far from
here?" I asked.

"It's near the place where we first arrived with the bus,
remember?" she replied.

"Ahh…Oh God, I do remember that bus journey! Oh, so it's not far away, good!" I felt calmer now. "So, explain to me again, what is happening?" I looked at my wife.

"Well…there is a big festival. It's a celebration of the music, traditions and lifestyle of the people who live in these parts. There is a show program, dancing, singing… a lot of stalls that people sell all types of goods… barbecues and picnics," she explained in a calm voice.

"Show program and food, sounds good to me!" I exclaimed with a huge grin quickly spreading across my face. "What do we need to do there when we arrive?"

"My parents have rented a stall, because they want to sell some of the home-made sweets and treats they've made. The only thing we need to do is help them carry all the jams and food to the festival," she said. "And that's it. They will take it from there… Me and you will just have food and enjoy the show and spend some quality time together," she finished.

"Sounds great!" I was happy.

Before I knew it, we were almost there. On the horizon, I witnessed a never-ending road off to the left, which was heavily occupied by multi-colored commercial stalls with decent-sized tables equipped with plastic roof tops for protection from the non-existent rain.

To the right, there was a freshly trimmed meadow drenched in a wild variety of pastel green colors, easily the size of a football field, if not bigger. The area was meticulously arranged with an indescribable number of wooden tables and benches. At the far-left side, in the distance, my eyes detected the barbecues and some of the food stalls that were slowly setting up shop.

The cherry on top was the big beautiful white stage, that was towering right behind the seating area.

"Oh wow! This is impressive!" my voice skipped.

"You haven't seen anything yet, dear! They haven't even started. All the people you see are just the vendors, who are here earlier to set up shop."

"I'm definitely looking forward to this!" I said with enthusiasm brewing in my voice.

We made our way to the stall that had been reserved by Kalina's parents, where we unpacked the trolleys and started to arrange the products in an appealing display on the table. Around half an hour later, the job was done.

Marko and Ginka started socializing with the people nearby. It looked like they knew each other from before; maybe vendors from a different village?
I was not sure.

"Ok, dear, they don't need our help anymore. Most of the stalls are full now, and people are starting to arrive. Let's go for a walk and see what they have to offer, sound good?" Kalina looked at me.

"Sounds great!" I said enthusiastically.

I honestly couldn't describe the sheer number of commercial stands that surrounded us. We started moving at a turtle's pace, requested by me, as I wanted to have a good look at all the goodies that were on offer. Everything imaginable was on those tables.

A stall displaying the latest fashion trends; tracksuits, hats, flip-flops, t-shirts, dresses and those little things that Ginka knits back in the house, which I couldn't remember the name of.

Next to it, another vendor offered candy of all types, flavors, colors and shapes.

A neighboring seller proffered hunting equipment, arrows, bows, knifes, camouflage clothing and fish bait.

At the next stall, there was a saleswoman whose table was overflowing with kids' toys; dolls, cars, tanks and every household item imaginable re-created in plastic form and shrunk to kids' size.

There were a truly bizarre combination of stalls one next to the other, and this pattern of commercial asymmetry continued for many yards down the road.

My eyes were all over the place as we casually strolled around. I was visually over-stimulated, as the colors and shapes were infinite.

Around 50 yards down the road, we turned to the right side and entered the green field. A huge stage that was dominating the center of the meadow was being looked after by a variety of professionals and sound engineers.
There was a substantial amount of space, that looked like an improvised dancefloor, between the main stage and all the rows of wooden tables.
It was obvious that some sort of concert would take place later on in the day.

"Oh…look at all those barbecues!"

At the far left of the stage, a row of food vendors were seductively waving me over with their tantalizing smoke signals.

"Let's go there!" I said hungrily.

"You don't want to look at some more knock-off American sports goods? Or buy sketchy imported candy, dear?" Kalina teased.

"No…I see meat from here!" I pointed to the barbecues.

We followed the trail of welcoming smells, stopping in front of a vendor with a substantial grill on a big sturdy table. All types of meat were sizzling and begging us to be picked.

An old man, wearing a flannel shirt with his sleeves rolled up, welcomed us with a big smile and a calm voice. My wife was doing all the talking with him, as I was mentally drooling all over the place.

"What is this called?" I interrupted her and pointed to some odd shaped meats.

"This is *kebabche*," she replied, pointing to a long piece of meat, shaped like a hot dog, dark brown in color with a few black stripes across created by the grill.

"And this is *kofte*," she explained, pointing at a flat meatball with the same color scheme. "I'll order you the combo meal," she said and gave instructions to the seller.

I was presented with a small-sized tray, with two long and two round pieces of meat, that I couldn't remember or pronounce the names of, a big scoop of red pesto, a piece of fluffy bread and a light sprinkling of green spices on top, all accompanied by a small plastic fork.

"That red scoop in the corner, is that the same thing I have every morning?" I asked Kalina, while still standing in front of the trader and waiting for our change.

"Yes, exactly."

"Great! I love that stuff!" I nodded. "I'm starving! Let's sit down and eat," I said as we headed to the tables not far away.

After some swift maneuvering around the increasing number of people, we were seated and ready to eat. I triumphantly took my plastic fork and stabbed it into the first piece of meat, took a serious bite and… boom! The flavor explosion that my taste receptors were forced to undergo was overwhelming.

I dipped the rest of the meat in the red pesto-like substance and took another bite. The second flavor ride was even better than the first one… What a rush of salty and meaty goodness! I tried to calm down the storm in my mouth with a few pieces of pale soft bread, that was acting as a host to all the green spices that were covering its entire surface.

"Oh! This is amazing!" I mumbled, stuffing my mouth like a hamster.

The whole festival area was getting busier by the second; cars were parking in the far distance, and buses were swooping in from left to right in the designated vehicle area, unloading battalions of thirsty and hungry festival goers. People of all ages ware invading the freshly-cut green pitch. Excitement and emotion were in the air, and a warm atmosphere was created out of thin air.

Minutes later, as we were facing the stage and enjoying our food, my wife informed me that the show program was about to begin in a few moments. I saw the technicians on stage, performing the final sound checks. People started rapidly gathering near the stage, as the spectacle was about to unfold very soon.

We were lucky enough to be on the first row of the benches and to have a perfect view of the high stage, so we just anchored ourselves to our location and prepared for the event.

The lights were on, the stage was empty, the crowd was poised with bated breath; it was time for the show to begin!

Introduction music, similar to an ethnic drum roll, started playing at a high volume from the speakers. All of a sudden, the audience burst into enthusiastic cheers.

A few moments later, a young male and female, probably in their early 20s, confidently walked out onto the stage with big smiles on their faces, each holding a clipboard. The young guy was sporting a relatively well-tailored black suit with a dark tie and pale shirt, while the girl was in an elegant and pretty red and white dress.

"Aha! These are the hosts for the show!" I said out of the blue.

"Not exactly," my wife responded. "These two kids will only greet everyone and announce the program for today. There are no hosts here."

"I understand," or at least this is what I said to Kalina, as having a show program without a host was confusing to me.

With a very professional and dynamic tone to their voices, the young couple earnestly greeted everyone and announced the official opening of the festivities.

After a quick wave of cheers from the crowd, the youngsters started reading from their clipboards, announcing the line-up and program for the day. At least this was what my wife was translating to me.

Abruptly, the couple on stage announced the first act in sync; well this is what I supposed, since they promptly left the stage and the casual music in the background quickly changed.

"Oh, I can't wait for the first performers, dear!" I exclaimed, buzzing with energy, as the music and the electricity from the people was contagious. "Who do you think it will be? Some famous rock band? Circus acts? Or a world-renowned stand-up comedian?" I asked my wife enthusiastically.

"Even better, dear!" she said, while extending her arm, pointing to the stage, and with perfect timing, introducing the next act.

The mob was cheerful and loud. By this point, they knew the line-up of performers and couldn't wait.

"Wow must be somebody really famous coming up! Look at that crowd! They are going crazy right now!" I was nervous to see who would grace the stage and rock the mic.

A shadow arose…followed by a body…a huge old man, the size of a wardrobe and the shape of a wine barrel, wobbled his way onto the stage.

"Who the hell is that? My God, look at the size of that mustache!" I yelled in shock.

"Oh, that is Kamen…" Kalina remembered, "the mayor. Oh my God, he is still mayor?!" she was questioning herself. "He started working when I was young and still living in the village. And yes, that is a well-groomed mustache, isn't it?" she agreed, looking at me.

The man was giving a vigorous and passionate speech. The crowd was responding to his every word. He was probably complimenting the magnificent people and the nature that grows in this part of the world. And in all fairness, I couldn't blame the guy; these were some outstandingly hard-working and friendly people, who were surrounded by some of the most vividly beautiful natural scenery I'd ever had the privilege to be exposed to.

After a few minutes, that magnificently sculpted dark mustache stopped moving as the mayor's speech came to a close. The festival was officially opened, and the actual show program was about to start.

I looked into my plastic tray and realized that all my food had migrated to my belly now.

"I need to go and re-fill, dear," I said with a big grin on my face, looking at my wife sitting next to me.

I jumped out of my seat and headed towards the nearest barbecue vendor.

I felt great! There was no sign of the terrible hangover that had been chasing me around the room early in the morning. Nothing was bothering me, not even the fact that I was surrounded by hundreds, maybe even thousands of strangers, and was part of an enormous crowd; something I'm usually terrified of.

Was it the food? The loving company of my wife? Or maybe the nature?

I was not sure, but one thing I did know...I liked this place! This was the first time a thought like that had danced through my mind. For the last few days, I had just looked at the village as a place where I was forced to stay for a period of time, smiling and exchanging pleasantries, but not really exploring the culture and seeing the perspective of the locals. Similar dialog were wrestling in my head as I very slowly made my way to the promised land that was filled with all types of meatballs and kebabs. The area was jam packed with people by this point, so it took ages to get near the food.

The music started playing, and something was happening on stage, but I couldn't focus on that, as I was skilfully navigating my way through the sea of faces and bodies that were here to enjoy the festivities.

I finally made it into the official waiting line for one of the vendors. After a few minutes, I was face to face with the gate keeper of heaven.

"How are you, my good man?" I was yelling at this jolly man, as the music was so loud, I could barely hear my own voice. "Three long thingies, two round thingies and a scoop of the red thingy!" I was gesturing very enthusiastically and pointing all over the grill, as my brain drew a blank, and I couldn't remember the proper names of all the foods.

Somehow the seller and I constructed a verbal bridge between us, and we managed to smash any linguistic challenges that were in front of us. He quickly placed all the requested food in another plastic try, accompanied with a fork and a few white napkins.

"Thank you, my good man!" I said, while digging into my pockets in the hope that I would have some notes and coins laying around, as this was the first time I'd actually needed to use any local money since I'd been here.

I handed over the currency I found, and he reliably returned the change I was due. The transaction was complete!

I wriggled my body though the ocean of people, and after a couple of minutes, I managed to reach the oasis that was our bench. I caught the first act mid-way through so my wife needed to fill me in on all the details I had missed.

"So, what is this then?" I asked.

"These are folklore dances, and all the performers are dressed in traditional folk costume," she explained as she pointed to the people on the stage.

A group of teenagers, four girls and four boys, were dancing with lightning-fast footwork to a variety of jumping rhythms. The clothing that they were wearing was absolutely mesmerizing; so colorful, embroidered, clean and presentable. I couldn't see the fine details from where I was sitting, as it was a bit too far for my eyes, but the performers definitely stood out. The only thing brighter than their clothing was their smiles; a permanent expression of happiness, joy and confidence. A scene to be witnessed!

After a few minutes of enthusiastic dancing, accompanied by very lively music, their performance came to a close as the boys vigorously stomped on the ground, and the girls yelled in a high-pitched voice. The music suddenly cut out, and they all took a bow... the crowd exploded!

"Wow, that was one hell of a dance!" I said to Kalina and took a bite from the delicious kebab.

"You haven't seen anything yet! Strap in! It's going to be a long ride!" she confidently noted.

As there was a few seconds' gap between the acts, I started to look around the green field. By this point it was covered with people. A lot of audience members were sitting on blankets and having picnics, since the area was massive and there was ample space for that.

The vendors were hustling and bustling, selling their goods, engaging in gossip, trading jokes and laughter with each other; or at least, this was how it appeared.

For some strange reason, there was a bit of empty space in front of the stage. Usually this is the best spot to watch a show, so I was surprised that it was empty, but before I got the chance to ask my wife the reason, the next act came on.

Suddenly, similar rhythmic background music started to play out of the sound system, and I witnessed a dozen tiny elderly women making their way to the center of the stage... The crowd started to applaud; I guessed they knew what was about to happen.

Twelve grandmothers formed a line, all wearing colorful, traditional folk garments. The crowd went quiet for a second, then the grandmothers, standing in front of the few microphones, started singing in absolute sync, and the audience started cheering again.

"This is interesting!" I yelled to my wife.

"Do you like it?" she replied.

"These women are probably in their seventies! And they are on stage performing like that, in front of a full crowd," I said. "Back home, we send our pensioners to Florida to live in retirement communities and to play Canasta all day…and here you turn them into superstars with bus-loads of adoring fans…interesting!" I said and took a substantial bite of one of the meatballs that was in my tray.

I noticed something that was strange… in the previous act, all the girls were wearing exactly the same clothing as each other, but in this case, the grandmothers were wearing different dresses.

"Why do the performers here wear different colors and types of costumes?" I asked my wife.

"Good question. Because each folk garb represents a different part of the country. The colors and the design are symbolic of that region, and in this case, you have four regions that are represented," she informed me.

"Oh, that is interesting…so just by looking at the colors and design, you know from which city and part of the country they're from?"

"Exactly!" my wife said.

"Oh, so just like football jerseys back home?" I fired.

"Err…well, not really, dear," my wife said, seeming confused.

"Yes, it's exactly like that! Each city has different colors and its own design, and when you see it, you know straight away where they come from…GO CHARGERS!!" I yelled, but it was so noisy, nobody even noticed me.

"I think that hangover is coming back now… What are you talking about?" Kalina asked, holding her head in disbelief.

"Of course it's the same, honey!" I was convinced. "Tell me how football and this is different? It's the same thing; each side is represented by a jersey, or a costume in this case; they play and perform in front of an enthusiastic crowd; and this is the favorite pass-time of the people," I finished.

Kalina started laughing, and with tears of joy in her eyes, managed to muster up a sentence. "In football, you have guys who are like 6'4", and are built like army vehicles versus singing grannies who are 4'11"

"Who are we rooting for then!" I asked and pointed. "I pick the blue team on the end," I announced, as I eyed the grandmothers in the navy colors.

My love chuckled and encouraged me to have a piece of meatball, so I would shut up for a bit.

The performance finished, the little grandmothers all took a bow and waved goodbye to the crowd… The audience cheered and yelled in appreciation of the magnificent singing.

It appeared to be intermission time, as people were relaxing, laughing, having food and taking it easy. Their attention was not needed at that moment.

Traditional ethnic sound waves were gently drifting from the huge dark speakers, providing a relaxing unobtrusive background noise. The baby-blue sky was so bright and beautiful that I was drawn to its appeal like a safety pin to a magnet. I tilted my head towards the sky and closed my eyes. The welcoming sun's rays kissed my face and body, the gentle breeze rocked my body back and forth, and the fresh air felt invigorating.

"Ah…I think I'm having one of those moments right now, that I've only hear hippies have…" I inhaled while speaking.

"You're truly happy!" Kalina exclaimed.

"Wow, that is a weird feeling…I think I like it!" I exhaled slowly, and sculpted a big smile on my face. "The love of my life is sitting next to me, I have fresh air in my hair, the sun on my shoulders, delightful food in my belly, the seductive music in my ears, and the intoxicating electricity of the crowd…What an experience! What a moment! Nothing can ruin my happiness…"

"James! James!" I was interrupted abruptly.

I forced my eyes open, and who was there, but none other than…

"Oh God, no! Drozdan…" I saw the tiny bald-headed man waving and making his way over to our table.

"Oh! Look who is coming, dear! Your new best friend, Drozdan. You must be excited to see him, right?" Kalina said, smiling.

"Please don't tell him I was happy…" I said seriously.

My wife was giggling. "He is so friendly and nice; I think he will be very pleased to find out."

"You don't understand; this man is a psycho! If he finds out I was happy, he will start congratulating and hugging me, talking about the universe, yoga and those goddamn chakras, you know?!" I was patting the air enthusiastically trying to explain.

"Hey, look who is here! Drozdan, we missed you! How are you?" Kalina sincerely expressed her joy when he was a few feet away.

"Hello sister!" the happy monk gave her a hug, as he approached our table.

I quickly noticed something odd.

"Oh God, Drozdan, why don't you have any shoes on? Why are you bare-footed?" I shook my head and pointed at his feet.

"I don't need shoes, you know…because mother nature is my provider of energy….and when I walk on her bare-footed, I get all the minerals I need, brother."

"Ugh…of course you do!" I was holding my forehead with my right hand and exhaling in disbelief.

"I will sit now!" he announced for some strange reason.

He quickly moved our plates to one side and sat on top of the table, rapidly adopting his favorite yoga pose…the lotus.

"Really! You gonna sit right in front of us in a hippie position…C'mon man!" I couldn't believe his audacity, as my heart rate started to go up.

Kalina thought it was cute and funny, as she was chuckling at this crazy man's mannerisms.

I stood up and scooped him off the table, then carried him to the seat that was available on the bench, unfortunately next to mine. I sat him down, as he resolutely displayed the lotus posture. Not making a move or vocalizing the weird situation, Drozdan just remained there with a huge happy grin on his face.

"Err…" I sat down next to him.

My wife was having so much fun at my expense. That was her free entertainment; me losing my shit over little things.

As her laughter subsided, she decided to spice things up again… by throwing in a verbal grenade. "So, Drozdan, you know James was happy today!"

"Oh!" the bizarre man gave me a sideways hug, leaning his fat potato head onto my shoulder and yelling, "I'm so happy that you're happy…how long were you happy for, brother?"

"Ugh…" I lowered my eyebrows and dropped my lips. "For about 20 seconds…" I muttered.

"Oh, that is great! What happened? So, you know… why weren't you a happy spirit for longer?" he asked, while still leaning on me.

"Err…never mind." I didn't want to hurt this well-meaning, crazy little man.

"Oh, that is great!" he was rambling. "What happened in your life that made you happy for 20 seconds?"

There is no way I was going to open up to him, definitely not now and not here, so I just replied, "It was the graceful mustache of your mayor!"

"Oh, that is a beautiful mustache, isn't it?" Drozdan said gently.

Kalina was vibrating with laughter at this point. She was stomping her feet and howling out loud. She gave me a side hug and leaned on my other shoulder.

Oh, what a scene to be witnessed; a middle-class, modest Californian journalist in his early 40s, thrown on to the other side of the planet with no idea where he was, being hugged by the woman of his dreams and also by a crazy spiritual bare-footed guru-type, who smelled like olives and ganja, with a bunch of meatball and kebab pieces on a plastic tray in front of him, surrounded by one of the craziest festivals ever!

As the intermission came to a close, I managed to free myself from the close intimacy that was overpowering my body.

"Ok…that's enough hugs for today, folks! Thank you!" I patted Drozdan and my wife on their backs…I wanted to enjoy a bit of my food, so I needed my hands to be free.

It was finally time for the next act! The crowd focused their attention, eagerly awaiting the next performers.

A slow drumbeat rattled the stage, followed by a towering man, dressed in traditional clothing; brown pants, a white shirt with ornaments, red vest and a brown hat. He was also sporting an intimidating mustache.

A few more men dressed in the exact same way approached the stage, some holding big or small drums, while others carried white bagpipes.
Everyone took their place and formed a colorful background, while all performing on their instruments.

The music suddenly stopped for a beat. There was an explosion of harmonized sound and a wild cheer rose up from the crowd… two boys and two girls rushed the stage!

Straight away, the dancing started; footwork so lightning fast and effortless that an American pro-boxer would be jealous. They were surging and jumping across the stage, performing a mesmerizing dance, resembling the mating call of exotic birds.

The girls ware portraying a story with their moves… playing hard to get, running away from the boys. The males ware thinking of ways to get their attention. Making gestures, smiling and talking to them. The girls were having none of it… They were dancing on the other side of the stage, flirtatiously looking at the opposite sex. The boys ware scratching their heads and talking to each other, plotting and thinking.

The men approached cautiously, as the music slowed down, and then the massive drum was the main sound provider. The guys both dropped to one knee, and enthusiastically started gesturing and clapping. They captured the female attention!

As the girls were giggling and looking innocent, they came forward to the center of the stage and started to dance and move around at a rapid pace.

The men looked at each other and patted themselves on the back. They'd managed to impress the girls! They clapped and jumped in the center, joining the girls. Everyone held hands and moved swiftly with hypnotic steps.

After a few moments, the music suddenly stopped, and all the performers took a quick bow… the crowd erupted once again. The act was complete. The story had been told via dance and music… what a storytelling skill these young people had.

I enjoyed the style of the ending of these dances and songs; they just cut off with no extra fluff or encore. The start was always very slow and dramatic, luring the audience, building up the anticipation… then the performance picked up speed. During the middle of the act, the audience was vibrating with energy, and then when the end comes…. boom! It just cuts off! Done!

As there was a small break between the performances, I wanted to get more information regarding the background of the dances, so I quizzed Kalina.

"What did I just see?" My eyebrows collided and I scratched my chin. "I mean, it looked like a play...a storytelling of some kind... Is it just me, or is there more to this?"

"These are traditional dances, retelling and romanticizing folk tales from back in the day. This particular dance tells the story of how a man can win over a girl," She gently gestured and explained. "You see, in these parts, the man needs to be worthy of a woman... because these women are tough as nails! So, the man needs to keep up with them, provide and work hard," she continued. "But also, they need to be caring, protective and fun in social situations. The dance represents a folk tale of how a young man can charm a young woman."

"Hold on!" I interrupted. "So, you need to be strong, protective, and fun in social situations?" I exclaimed. "So how in hell did I win you over then?"

"Magic!" Kalina laughed.

"I can't even handle the alcohol in these parts," I was shaking my head. "I don't know what you see in me!" I joked.

"You are a kind soul! I see a free spirit trapped in a corporate body...my brother," Drozdan whispered in my left ear out of nowhere.

"Oh!" I quickly pulled my head away. I had completely forgotten that he was sitting next to me. "I don't even know how to react to that...Somebody please play some music; it's getting awkward in here!" I shouted at the stage.

A fast drum started pounding murderously, and the speakers were vibrating... Another performance was about to grace the stage. The tempo got more intense by the second… everyone fell quiet… holding their breath in anticipation.

A middle-aged man with precise steps steadily moved towards the center… slowly beating the big drum that he was holding. As the background noise was getting more and more robust, a second man appeared, dressed exactly the same way; white shirt, red cummerbund and brown pants. There was the same movement, expression and rhythm coming from his drum. Both men were identical, like two drops of water.

A young male hastened onto the stage, clothed like the other two men, with a beautiful waistcoat and holding a little red handkerchief in his right hand. He started to jog in circles, chased by the drummers; a dance that they'd been doing thousands of times. At this point, the pace of the music slowed down substantially.

The two drummers positioned themselves in the center of the stage, putting their drums down and still slapping them every second, creating a slow-paced rhythm.

From both flanks was a slow invasion… four men, two from each wing, approached the spotlight and started performing traditional moves in a synchronized manner, all adorned in the same folk garments.

Two men provided a surge of clarinet sounds, flooding the area. The tempo of dance and music was still slow, but you could sense that things were picking up speed.

The dancers displayed their skilful footwork, while the two drummers stepped back into the shadows of the main stage, trying not to hijack the attention from the main performers, who were enjoying the spotlight. The two clarinet players that were on the side lines slowly joined the drummers in the darkness.

The music suddenly stopped for two seconds as everyone on stage froze… An unstoppable mixture of thunderous bagpipes combined with a lively rush of clarinet sounds slashed the air… the intimidating drums invaded the mix of sounds. The tempo was fierce and loud. A few seconds later, the ground was shaking, and the vibrations were working their way through my body… The screams and the music gave me goose bumps… the hair on the back of my neck was fervently saluting the skies.

"What the hell is happening?!" my brain was screaming.

Then the singer arrived! A middle-aged, blond woman, wearing a beautiful traditional costume in white and navy-blue colors with gold ornaments and a little dark hat, enthusiastically charged the stage, holding a microphone.

The previous powerful minutes that I'd experienced were only the build-up to the actual beginning of the performance! Open arms, a big smile and a few leaps were all it took for her to take absolute command of the stage. A beautiful voice started preaching to the people… telling the story of the region and the lifestyle. At least that was how I saw things.

The men were dancing all around, gripping each other by the arms, moving adeptly back and forth, one of them holding and spinning a traditional piece of fabric.

Having finished a verse, the singer joined the men in the dance… everyone was moving so effortlessly, gliding across the center of the stage.

Then, it was time for her to sing again, so everyone made space, and the stage was hers once more.

All of a sudden, as the cheerful rhythms flirted with the crowd, a small number of female dancers started appearing from the shadows; ten girls in two rows of five slowly occupied the background space. These girls were dressed immaculately, their costumes covered in intricate details that I could barely distinguish from a distance. White, green and red were the main contenders in this color exhibition.

The view was absolutely astonishing. A completion was reached as a wild mix of colors, clothing and instruments dominated the floor at this point. Still, in all of this synchronized chaos, confidently overpowering the center stage.... the main star, the performer with the most beautiful singing voice I'd ever heard, was proclaiming her truth to a legion of adoring supporters.

On both sides of the huge stage, the two groups of five girls started holding hands and dancing in circles. The men, still with their arms around each other, were moving back and forth with their feet only.

The second verse was over, and the performer joined the circle on the right side, then started dancing with the young girls... For a middle-aged woman and a singer, she had tremendous speed and agility.

As the tension and vivacity sharply increased, reflected by the music, it was clear that the final verse was coming up. The drum sounds were ferociously beating down, and the rhythms became intense.

The crowd hadn't stopped clapping and roaring for the last four minutes.

The singer stepped back as the two men holding and banging the massive drums put them down in the center of the stage and closed them together.

A few seconds later, with the help of a backup dancer, the singer was lifted on top of the drums and was standing in a very dominant position. She had her hand high in the sky, whilst singing at the top of her lungs. The clarinet players were on one knee, playing in her direction, resembling Indian gurus trying to hypnotize a venomous king cobra snake.

The men were dancing all around, as the women were in the background, trying not to distract the audience with their beauty. The unique combination of sounds created by all these instruments had a deeply emotional impact on all the people around, as everyone was completely filled with energy, joy and smiles… A story about their culture and way of life told in the form of a powerful musical performance.

I felt it, even though I didn't understand the lyrics or the meaning of the dances… The constant wave of goosebumps were no coincidence.

The final moments were getting more and more intense; the conclusion in the form of a powerful eruption was about to occur very soon. The singer's voice was dynamic and firm, yet gentle and welcoming. While still standing on top of the two big drums, she clenched her hand, forming a fist, which she proudly raised in the air, delivering her final vocals… The men increased their speed of dancing in time with the music.

The crowd was singing along at full volume… and a few seconds later… the final words were delivered, with a loud sound, resembling a "HEY!" The music cut off… the audience lost it… the place was a madhouse… they loved it! So did I!

A cataclysm of cheers and roars were all propelled towards the stage… the targets of the ovations took a bow.

"OH MY GOD!" I exhaled. "Are you kidding me?! This was…amazing!" I was gasping for air. "This music is so powerful! It's unbelievable…right?"

I turned towards Kalina, whose eyes were filled with tears. She was quietly crying. I had been absorbed in the show on stage, so I hadn't even noticed.

"Oh, dear…why are you crying, are you ok?" I asked her.

"Sometimes I miss my home…," she replied as the tears became heavy.

"Oh, my love, I'm so sorry!" I panicked and didn't know what to say. I hugged her, and she buried her head in my chest.

All of a sudden, Drozdan who was sitting next to me and who hadn't said a single word during the performance jumped up, stating, "Oh, I love group hugs!" and gave me a hug from the back. To top it all off, he leaned his head against my upper back.

"Err…God damn it!" I grunted.

"Is Drozdan giving you a hug right now? And that makes you feel uncomfortable?" my wife asked, while I was still holding her weeping face close to my chest.

"Yes!" I said, puffing.

"That is funny!" my love said, while sobbing and chuckling at the same time.

Kalina lifted her head, wiped her tears and fixed her hair.

"Thank you for the support. I love you," she whispered.

"I love you!" I said out loud.

"Oh, that's so sweet, James! I love you too!" Drozdan yelled, while still leaning against my back.

I made a quick ninja move and managed to escape the claws of the happy monk. I needed an excuse to stand up and walk around, as I was feeling sore.

"Let's see how my parents are doing and how business is going!" Kalina suggested.

Jackpot! Exactly what I needed!

"Yes, great idea!" I jumped up and grabbed my wife by the hand.

"I'll come with you!" Drozdan said.

"Err…" I didn't want him to come, so I improvised. "Oh, you know what… you'd better stay here and guard the table."

"Guard the table?" he questioned, tilting his head to one side.

"Yeah you know…" I panicked. "This table is our temple of happiness, you see…" Kalina was giving me a weird look. "What if evil souls want to infiltrate our spiritual stronghold… and corrupt our hearts." I had no idea what I was saying, but I knew I needed to speak in a way he would understand. "Oh yeah, and if those evil souls take over this table…they will impose a new regime…." I enthusiastically gestured all over the place.

"A new regime?" His pupils grew wide.

"Yes! A new regime…They will take away your ganja, and make you wear leather dress-shoes!" I was slapping the table and being loud.

"Oh no! I hate dress shoes!" The happy monk looked shocked. "And you know what…they will force you to meditate in dress-shoes…Can you meditate in dress shoes? Well can you?!" I was giving an Oscar-worthy performance.

"I can't meditate in them!" Drozdan was shaking his head. "I hate dress shoes…They are only for corporate shills!"

I drastically slowed down the pace of this bizarre exchange. I leaned in and quietly said to his face, "Drozdan…are you a corporate shill? Do you contribute to the money-hungry, soul-steeling villains who rule the capitalistic machine?"

"Oh…no, it's not possible! I don't give money to them in any form! I don't buy their products!" Drozdan was shaking his head again.

I looked at him and said, "Well…you did buy a fridge, didn't you?"

Drozdan froze with his mouth wide open, contemplating whether he did indeed contribute to the thing he hated the most...corporatism.

"That should give us half an hour," I chuckled and grabbed my wife by the hand.

She seemed upset, as she didn't always appreciate my unorthodox sense of humor.

"Don't be mean to him!" Kalina frowned. "He just wants to be your friend, and he means well."

"I know…I know," I wobbled my head and felt a bit guilty.

Fortunately for me, I didn't have much time to reflect on what had happened or let my guilt settle in, because we quickly made our way to the long road that was covered with the endless commercial stalls, selling everything you could possibly imagine; knock-off branded clothing, dark colored hunting gear, colorful sweets, traditional souvenirs, fluffy ice cream, fake leather jackets and much more. Every stall was viciously competing for the attention of the potential clients passing by.

Once again, my eyes were overwhelmed and swiveling all over the place, like a child entering a candy store. I wanted to see and touch everything!

We slowly headed towards the space that was occupied by Ginka and Marko. Getting there was not an easy task, as I stopped at multiple stalls. My curiosity was killing me.

After about ten minutes, we reached my wife's parents table. They started chatting and looking at the amount of sales that they had accumulated so far.

The show program was at full blast, providing a pleasant background noise to my inner thoughts and observations.

Most of the people had devoted their full attention to the stage that hosted a number of similar acts, dances, songs and comedy sketches, all in the native language, telling the story of the rich cultural heritage the region possessed.

A few people were still wandering about on the road, jumping from vendor to vendor, like little buzzing bees looking for fresh flowers. The time was steadily passing by, as the sun started to hide away behind the horizon, and the show was nearing its culmination. The love of my life informed me that we needed to head back to our table, which was fatefully being guarded by Drozdan.

As we were walking back, I asked my wife, "So, what did your parents say…How are the sales?... Did the people like the cookies and jam?!"

"They are the hit of the festival!" Kalina's voice catapulted. "They sold almost everything!"

"That is great to hear!" I said calmly.

We sat back at our table, where I looked at Drozdan and said, "Any evil spirits trying to sit here while we were gone?"

"Only a few...but I chased them away!" he said proudly.

We settled in for the end of the show, as there was a short pause and an announcement that signalized a grand performance was about to begin, or this is how I perceived it, as people started clapping and whistling loudly.

The stage was brightly lit, as the darkness had firmly positioned itself in the sky above. The extravaganza was about to begin!

Suddenly, the first wave of familiar ethnic sounds, which were impossible to put into words, spilled over and showered the crowd. The cheers started at a prolonged methodical pace, accompanied by an escalating amount of noise. Four small children started to invade the stage from both sides, all immaculately dressed in traditional costumes; brown pants, colorful folk footwear, dark red waistcoat, white shirt embroidered with red customary ornaments, burgundy and brown coat, and a dark hat. Each was proudly holding a large white bagpipe with three wooden pipes.

The boys were young, no more than seven or eight years of age, but they were playing the instruments with such professionalism and a strong captivating stage presence that the crowd was hypnotized by their performance.

Only a few short moments later, and the youngsters were forced to share the spotlight with someone new, which just added to this sound masterpiece.

From the shadows, six teenagers, all males dressed in the exact same way and behaving in the same manner, were slowly making their entrance. Everyone was positioned at the front part of the massive and deep stage, slowly pacing back and forth, controlling the crowd and spellbinding them with a slow and steady serenade of the native bagpipes under the delicate guidance of their masters.

It wasn't really possible to focus on the back part of the stage, as the lights were off, so only the males at the front were visible. At this point, the majority of the performers were calming down. The boys were producing slow and gentle sounds from the traditional instrument that they were gripping.

All of a sudden… An explosion of roaring bagpipe sounds blasted all over the area! The lights at the back part of the stage went up, so you could see everything. It was a setup! Rows of bagpipe players were standing there; so many, I couldn't count them all.

There was a fearless platoon of intimidating men and women, all decorated in a spectacular way from head to toe, blowing and channeling all of the musical energy into the dead animal skin in their hands, creating a powerful sound epopee, that was echoing all over the area. The slow, peaceful performance of the innocent children was over. It was time for war!

A loud synchronized blast of sounds hit the ground. The sky was shattered, and the grass became stiff as hammer nails. Everything was shaking. Hearts ware racing, minds were blown, memories were created, and an intense wave of emotion was mercilessly crashing over the bodies of the screaming and cheering fans.

A vicious chain of adrenaline bricks were hitting my body. Goosebumps were crawling all over me, and my heart was bouncing inside my chest... What a rush!

The musical beat-down of the innocent continued! Another surge of powerful ethnic vibrations quickly snowballed towards the audience, who were by now shaken to the core. All the performers took a deep breath, and just a moment later, a powerful wave of bagpipe sounds erupted again all over the place.

The emotional roller coaster continued. There was no mercy for anyone. At this point, everyone, including the vendors, were captivated by the unbelievable performance on stage.

The music became even more intense as the tempo increased. The atmosphere became red hot, as the crowd was cheering and loudly whistling.

Suddenly, a large man, the size of a building, with a muscle structure resembling an armored suit, with a long dark beard and a stylish long, thick mustache, confidently stepped on stage. He was easily above six feet, something that was rare for these parts, all dressed in traditional clothing, with his sleeves rolled up so you could see his giant forearms, and he had two medium-sized swords tucked in his waistcoat. He was slowly pacing back and forth at the front part of the stage, while in the background, the numerous bagpipe players ware slashing the clouds and engraving the mountains with their powerful performance.

The man stopped smack in the middle of the stage, looking at the crowd, commanding their attention, while the background music was becoming more and more intense.

He fearlessly pulled out one of the swords that was tucked away and raised it proudly with his right hand. In a deep manly voice, he started slowly reciting some sort of a poem or a mantra.

As the moments passed, the crowd was becoming more and more emotional. They were hanging on to his every word. The music that was playing in the background made his message even more powerful. His deep… steady… voice was shaking the ground! A powerful… BOOM! BOOM! BOOM!

Fireworks…eccentrically blasting away behind the stage, glowing like a rising phoenix in the dark sky!

The speech ended as everyone's faces were glowing in different colors from the pyrotechnics, mostly green, red, orange, and white. The bagpipe players finished their performance as the crowd wildly cheered them on. Then the lights went off, so they could make an unnoticed escape.

The colorful explosions in the sky were now the main attraction; a glowing sensation of the genius creation of the Chinese signaled the end of the program.

After a minute, the fireworks ran out of steam and petered out. Everyone was emotional and overwhelmed with joy. They couldn't hide it, as it was visibly written on their faces. It took a minute or so for the crowd to come back down from that adrenaline mountain that they'd just climbed.

The stage lights came back on again, but the podium was empty, without any sign of the previous performances at all. Quiet yet cheerful music started playing. On stage stepped that glorious mustache, faithfully carried by the mayor of the village.

That big tub of happiness rolled around to the microphone stand and made a few announcements and a quick closing statement. A colossal surge of applause immediately followed. All the ovations and admiration for the spectacular extravaganza, that it had been a privilege to witness for the last few hours, were well deserved. The official entertainment program was complete!

People all around were visibly pleased, trading glowing grins, positive roars and pleasantries with one another. A cheerful vibe was pulsating all over the field.

Some of the vendors who had managed to sell everything they had to offer started to slowly pack their bags and eventually leave. This was the case for Marko and Ginka. As it turned out, their stall had been a commercial mega success, as they had completely sold out of all the jam, cookies and cakes they had prepared. But in all fairness, the old woman had some immaculate cooking skills, so such a victory was not surprising, not one bit.

It was getting very cold now, as the nights around these parts could be freezing to the bone. We decided it was time to leave. We said goodbye to Drozdan, who started to meditate on the table and listen to the relaxing quiet music that was still playing from the half-lit stage.

We helped Kalina's parents with the packing, then we headed home. I was feeling very tired. The day had started with a terrible hangover, and then I had been put on an emotional rollercoaster with the performance program I had experienced.

After fifteen minutes of slow-paced walking and chatting, accompanied by laughter and a few smiles from all sides, we reached the house. We put all the trolleys away and went inside.

It was late and I was tired and still full of food from the meat fiesta that my taste buds had undergone. I took a speedy shower and changed into my pajamas. Everyone went upstairs to have some tea and to chat. I was not able to, as my worn-out body was begging me to go to bed.

I hugged my wife and said goodnight to everyone. A few moments later, I was in my bed. With my eyes half open and barely conscious, I mumbled, "Oh…what a day!"

I quickly fell asleep.

# 07.26.1985 (Friday)

I was woken up by the deafening screeching that our rooster and Drozdan's pet were creating, but this time I was not bothered or angry at them. I calmly opened my eyes, and after a few moments, I raised from the bed, sitting on the edge of the firm mattress, gathering my thoughts and energy.

I made my way to the adjacent kitchen and filled up a big sturdy glass with cold water, throwing a few slices of freshly cut lemon inside.

"Ah! This will do for now," I said to myself as I took the first sip.

Next door, in the other guest room, I could hear the family chatting. I needed a moment to myself before I could enter the vocal jungle next door, so I went out onto the little terrace. As the sun was rising up from his sleep, a warm golden glow was thrown onto the area, swathing my whole body.

I stood on the balcony looking at the scenery in front of me.

An unexpected stream of inner sadness ran through me.

"Why do I feel sad?" I muttered. "It's my last day here…We are leaving in a few hours. I should be happy! When I first came here, I wanted to leave straight away. Why do I feel this way?" I continued, quietly mumbling to myself. "Back in the States, I live in a great house with the love of my life. I have a good career, beyond average living standards, and we often socialize in the best restaurants and piano bars San Diego has to offer." I was perplexed. "Why am I already missing this tiny village… God damn it!" I was angry at myself.

I had everything back home, yet somehow the fact that life would go on for these villagers without me, and the fact that I wouldn't be a part of it drove me up the wall.

How could such a primitive settlement with such a slow and unsophisticated lifestyle leave such a mark on me? "I should be happy that I'm leaving!" I punched the air. "Ah…damn it!" I exhaled.

I took another sip from my drink, throwing a quick peek at the picturesque mountains covered with lush forests, then decided to go and join the family in the next room.

I opened the door of the main guest room and saw everyone smiling and laughing, as they were having breakfast and enjoying each other's company.
Everyone was happy to see me, as they beamed glowing grins at me. Even though I was feeling sad and frustrated, my iron guard collapsed, as the sheer warmth that they had all showed me over the last few days made me smile and slightly chuckle.

"Hey…come and have breakfast, dear," Kalina said cheerfully.

I sat down next to her and prepared myself a few pieces of toast with that lovely red pesto stuff, then I stole a variety of salami and a few pieces of cheese from the big plates at the center of the table.

After half an hour or so, breakfast was finished, and my wife informed me that our bus was leaving in a few hours, so we needed to pack our bags and go.

She gathered all of her belongings that were in her bedroom, and we both met with all the empty suitcases in the small guest room where I was residing.

As we were both packing our bags, my wife was talking, but I wasn't really paying attention this time, as I was once again trapped in my own head. I couldn't shake off that feeling of sadness that had washed over me again. Why was I feeling that way? I knew I could never stay and live in this place, but on the other hand, I would miss the people and their lifestyle.

After half an hour of packing, we were done. We got dressed up, then it was time to leave for the bus stop, which was fifteen minutes away. Kalina's parents were waiting for us downstairs. As we started dragging the suitcases along, I took a final look around the room that I'd spent the last few days in. I would definitely miss that place.

We joined my wife's parents, then slowly started marching towards the improvised bus stop; the same place where we'd first arrived a few days ago.

We were chatting, breathing in the fresh air and enjoying the sun, when all of a sudden, I stopped. I couldn't help myself.

"I just need a minute. You guys keep walking. I will catch up with you," I said to my wife.

"Is everything ok?" she asked.

"Yes, everything is fine… I just need to do something," I replied.

They continued on, and I headed to Drozdan's house. I don't know why, but I couldn't bear the idea that he would probably go to Ginka's house later on and find out that I'd left and would probably never see me again. I needed to say goodbye at least.

A few moments later, I was at his place, standing in front of the big solid red door. After a few knocks, he opened and greeted me with a big smile and a rehearsed phrase, *"Namaste.* I'm so happy to see you my brother…" Drozdan went for a hug, but I swiftly ducked and stood back up.

"Hey…listen, buddy, I just want to say, it was nice meeting you, and I wish you all the best…" I extended my palm for a handshake.

"Are you going somewhere, brother?" he asked, tilting his head.

"Oh, yes…I'm leaving the village, as me and Kalina are going to a city up north to visit her friends from the time she was a student. We are going to stay there for a few days, and then we are flying back to California," I explained.

"Oh," a sad expansion appeared on the happy monk's face. "Well…you know, your deeds and kindness will live in these lands forever." His smile came back to life, as that never-ending optimism filled up his body once again.

"I'm just leaving; I'm not dying you know!" I chuckled.

"You are a good man, James! A bit more enlightenment in your life, that's what you need…but a good man indeed."

Drozdan surprised me with a jump hug that I couldn't outmaneuver this time. After an awkward minute with him, that felt more like an hour, I waved goodbye and started walking towards Kalina.

"Damn, I'm going to miss that crazy little bastard!" I mumbled with a big smile.

A few moments later, I caught up with the rest of the family, who were just a few yards away.

"Hey, did I miss anything?" I asked my wife.

"Oh, that is so cute, stopping at Drozdan's house to say goodbye…You going to miss him?" my love teased.

I felt unconformable and tried to hide what had really happened, and replied, "Err…no, no, I needed to return a…" my eyes started to wander as I was walking, "…bottle opener, you know? He lent me one, and I needed to return it, that's all." I was not convincing.

"Yeah…a bottle opener, I get it," Kalina winked at me and gave me a gentle stroke on the arm.

After ten minutes or so, we arrived at the tiny improvised bus stop. A familiar fat face was prancing around the bus in a stylish track suit; the same Formula 1 wannabe who had bounced us from side to side like sacks of potatoes in his metal box of death on our way here. I was not excited to see this behemoth.

Marko took our luggage and started talking with the driver as he opened the lower compartment of the bus, which was used for storage, and helped him put our bags away.

Kalina was hugging her mother, laughing and slightly crying at the same time. She was overcome with emotions, knowing that the next time she would see her would be years from now. Then she did the same with her father, who had really opened up to me over the last few days.

The time was flying by, and before we knew it, it was time to board the bus and leave for the northern part of the country.

My heart was beating fast and my stomach was in a knot. I didn't know why, but I was short of breath and couldn't think straight. It felt like I was having a panic attack; I didn't know what was happening.

Ginka gave me a big strong hug and a kiss on the cheeks. Marko looked at me, smiled and gave me a firm handshake, then pull me in and patted me on the back. He looked at Kalina and I, smiled, nodded his head and gave us a thumbs up. My wife was wiping tears of joy from her cheek bones. I gave her a hug, then she leaned her head on my chest, and I kissed her on the forehead. She was happy that we were all together, even though the next time could be a decade from now.

Both of her parents were looking at us with approving eyes. I had been accepted; I was part of the family now! My stress was gone!

This intimate and emotional moment was rudely interrupted by the obese driver, who in a loud voice signaled that it was time for everyone to board the bus, as we were about to leave.

Final hugs and kisses were exchanged before we boarded the vehicle. We sat at the very back where, from the huge window, we could see Ginka and Marko, who were waving and smiling at us. As the driver took his time to adjust his music, make himself comfortable and get himself ready, we had a few moments before we drove off.

When I sat down, I reached into my right pocket to search for some mints, but instead I pulled out a red medal. I opened my palm and showed it to Kalina.

"This is the medal your father gave me the other day, when I was on the terrace with him!" I exclaimed. "Did you ask him the reason why he gave it to me?"

Kalina slowly put her hand on top of the metal symbol and said, "Bravery comes in many different shapes, sizes and professions. Not everyone can do what you do, and not everyone can do what my father has done. He gave you this medal, because in his eyes you are worthy of it; you are brave. It takes courage to open your heart to the unknown, to travel to the other side of the globe and to jump into a different culture with traditions and a language you don't know anything about.

"You eventually opened up to him, and he opened up to you, both in your own ways. For him, you are brave and worthy, never forget that…You are smart as a fox, but you hide your emotions from the outside world. You don't let anybody see your vulnerabilities…just like him.

"He knows that you will take care of me and our family. When he looks at you, he sees himself… if he was born at a different time and in a different place…"

My eyes were wide open, and my eyebrows were reaching for the ceiling. I could not believe that he had such an opinion about me; I was deeply moved.

The engine of the bus started roaring. We were about to leave in a few seconds. I turned around and saw Marko and Ginka smiling and waving at us. At that moment, I realized that I had just received the approval that I'd never got from my own parents… I had been accepted by people who I could barely communicate with.

My wife turned around and said, "So…Mr. James Elmswood…what do you think of my tiny village?"

"These were the most fascinating few days of my life! I love you!" I hugged her and gave her a kiss… Then we settled down and got ready to travel up north to visit the town where she had spent her college years.

The End

# About The Author

First of all, thank you so much for making it to the end and reading my book!

I hope you had a fun and enjoyable time reading my work.

Second, this is the part where I need to talk about myself: I'm just a cheeky Bulgarian bloke, who came to the UK as a young adult. Ended up falling in love with the people, the accents and the chips.

I've been living in the UK for a while now and I call Liverpool my home.

I write about different topics and I want to expand my skills as much as possible. Also, recently I started writing comedy and I even managed to do a couple of sets in a comedy club here in Liverpool.

I'm a very ambitious and creative fella, and I'm always up to something, expect more book and non-book related stuff from me in the future and thank you for being a part of the journey.
Shameless website plug, below:

www.mikeyanek.com

Thank you for reading and see you soon!

# Final Note

Thank you so much for reading this book!
I hope you found the content fun and
enjoyable.

I also have a blog where I write on different
topics:

www.mikeyanek.com

And if you can do me a favour and leave a
review for this book, if you think I did a good
job, it will really help boost its credibility.

Thank you in advance.

P.S.
And while I have you here, on the next page
you can check out some of my other books.

# OTHER BOOKS
---
# BY MIKE YANEK

**2017** | **The Book of Manly Quotes:**
200 Quotes on Masculinity, Success and Happiness

**2018** | **Just Do It - Damn It**
The Approach to Life, Business & Success

**2019** | **Warrior Cultures of the World:**
Samurai, Immortal, Spartan, Maori

**2019** | **The Book of Manly Quotes Part 2:**
200 Quotes on Leadership, Warfare & Love